ONLY AFTER DARK

One Man's Descent into Obsession and Madness

Thomas H Murray

BASTET PUBLISHING

TABLE OF CONTENTS

CHAPTER ONE

How I love the wild winter waves crashing at my feet! My 'love' is not like others who really mean 'like', as in "I really love your hair". No, when I love, it is with such intensity and passion that it overwhelms me. I completely surrender to its power.

That is why I ended up in Estoril, Portugal, sitting on the Paredão, the paved pedestrian pathway along the ocean, one winter night in the beginning of January. It was right after my first depressing Christmas alone without my wife, who totally crushed me with her many-year affair with my close friend. As they say, there is a fine line between love and hate. My emotions would flip between raging hatred to sorrowful yearning every few minutes. I was losing my mind.

After years of abuse, she finally pushed me over the line. I resurrected a shred of self-respect and divorced her. Fleeing to the distracting strangeness of a foreign country, I chose Portugal almost randomly, but I chose Estoril, because it fit exactly into my state of mind. Decaying and decrepit manor houses of forgotten nobility and palaces of long-dead, exiled kings populated the town.

These once grand edifices had decayed almost beyond recognition. Sections of walls with old blue and white tile scenes of a long-lost courtly life were now covered in spray-painted graffiti, the symbols of revolution and anarchy. Grand staircases missing marble steps that had fallen to the overgrown gardens below. Windows and doors were mostly bricked up to prevent the drug-addled derelicts from creating their dens there.

Yet the intrepid could usually find a way to enter only to discover even worse decay within the moldy walls. Furniture from a fashion of generations ago stood thickly covered in dust. Marble busts had taken on the patina of those normally found in cemeteries. Darkened portraits stared from the walls like evil phantoms. The stale air smelled like the last exhalations of long dead corpses.

Jagged graffiti of the recent peaceful democratic revolution, ending over forty stifling years under the dead hand of the fascist followers of Salazar, covered the town walls. The Socialists and the Communists started a new experiment in democracy. Repairing the grande dames of a long-past expired time was not a priority of the new regime.

You may ask how I ended up living in the palace of the expired exiled Romanian king Carlos II? I wanted to be by the ocean and close to Lisbon. I started by taking the train from Cais de Sodre in Lisbon to the end of the line in Cascais. The quaint fishing village was a playground for the last kings of Portugal. It, too, was full of decaying, rubble-strewn manor houses. The problem with Cascais was that the harbor water smelled like a cesspool. I could not possibly sit for long enjoying the sea air.

I continued my search by visiting the next station on the way back to Lisbon. Monte Estoril had the same state of decay, but the water still smelled putrid. The next stop was Estoril. As one exited the station, Europe's grandest casino stood beyond an extensive park of faded defunct fountains and palm trees that had not been trimmed in years with their dead brown fronds hanging down like hula skirts. The casino had managed to stay open, but clearly had no money for keeping up appearances.

Just to the left of the park heading towards the casino was the Deck Bar, a local institution from the late 1920's, where one could sit outside under a wonderful canopy of trees and gather one's thoughts. My thoughts coalesced around Estoril being my new home.

I ordered a glass of wine and asked the only waiter who could speak English if he knew of anyone who was renting an apartment nearby. He told me of an elderly man who still lived in the palace of the exiled Romanian king, who had died already twenty-five years before. The caretaker was the only one of the once many camp-followers and courtiers who remained loyal to old King Carlos.

This last loyalist was trying to keep the old palace from crumbling into the brown weeds that once was a beautiful garden. He would certainly like some help with that. Besides, he had not been paid for his services since 1953.

The waiter gave me the address and directions. I walked the ten minutes to a once imposing green gate that was surrendering to the rust that held it in its deadly grip. An enormous pine tree nearly blocked the view of a once majestic palace. The cobbled pathway was nearly invisible by the weeds growing up between the stones.

I carefully opened the gate, not wanting to push it off its hinges. Luckily, someone had forgotten to lock it. Approaching the Doric columns bracketing the steps up to the tall door, tall enough for a man on horseback to enter, I took in what age had done to it.

Besides the once grand entrance, every other hole was imperfectly bricked up with gaps and cracks throughout. The swimming pool, just visible from the front steps, had become a brackish pond. Waist-high weeds and wild plants reclaimed the once beautiful gardens.

Just as I was about to rap the great brass door knocker, tarnished by the nearby salty sea air, I thought to myself how this was exactly what I was looking for. This derelict ruin exactly fit my state of mind. I would feel right at home. I hoped the interior would be the same.

The Deck Bar in Estoril, still going strong.

After rapping on the door for some minutes, a small old man, as decrepit as the palace, answered. I explained my purpose and to my great relief, he spoke perfect English with a slight Eastern European accent. He was excited to see me and invited me in. We sat on old worn sofas in the parlor. Before us was an enormous marble fireplace that one could walk into. On the hand-painted wallpaper hung ink drawings of various grandees in poses of martial courage.

High above us was a glass ceiling that revealed all manner of detritus that had fallen on it. Yet, it still let in enough light to just make out the details of my surroundings. He disappeared into the large dining room through the double doors opposite the parlor's entrance. There were two grand dining tables that filled almost the entire dining room. I considered the wonderful feasts that room must have had in its heyday.

My host disappeared into another room further in that must have been the kitchen. After some minutes he reappeared with a tray of espressos and stale cookies. Setting the tray down before us, he started to explain.

The old man only had enough energy to do minimal upkeep of the place. He had been living there since when the King went into exile in 1940 following the coup of the Nazi Iron Guard that placed his son Michael on the throne. Being the king's valet allowed him to know the king well. He had been living in the same rooms off to the side of the dining room's kitchen for over thirty-five years.

I introduced myself, leaving out the recent tragedy of my marriage, the real reason I was there at all. I was an author who had hit a long dry patch and needed to change my environment to find my muse again. Explaining that I had some money from royalties of past books, I did not need to take a job. My work was writing, and this old palace would be the perfect place to find my inspiration.

He laughed politely and showed me the rooms he lived in. They were the only livable ones left. All the other rooms were locked up. They had not seen the light of day since 1953 when the king died and everyone else drifted off to other shores. Occasionally, he would

Thanksgiving dinner 2019 in the palace dining room.

mutter something under his breath. I asked him to speak up. He replied that he was just talking to the spirit of the king as he did every day for twenty-five years, but not to worry. The king only showed himself to his faithful valet.

I decided to play along with the addled oldster and asked how the king would take to a new interloper living there. He told me not to worry. He would explain everything to His Highness, and there would be no problem at all. I told him jokingly that we would have to put a clause into the lease that if the king did not take kindly to me living there that I could break the lease.

He agreed with a grave voice, telling me to write up whatever lease with any clause that I wanted. I asked him why he was in such a hurry to leave after so much time. He had a sister in New York who managed to obtain a visa for him to live there. If he did not take this chance, he may never have another one.

I supposed that was a good enough answer. As for me, I was enamored with the idea of living in a palace, even if it was almost in ruins. What American would not?

His rooms consisted of a bedroom, living room, bathroom, and a kitchen; perfect for a solitary soul looking for somewhere to disappear, hoping to put the jigsaw puzzle of his life back together. It had stable electricity, and hot water for showers and the radiators to keep the winter damp away. He had turned all that off everywhere else.

The apartment was nicely furnished with full bookshelves, a decent desk looking out onto the overgrown garden, and a long glass and iron dining table. The kitchen was fully stocked and complete.

We returned to the parlor, where we had our coffee. He gave me a piece of paper and pen and told me to write down the terms to agree on. The lease would be only half a page and the terms he proposed were the following:

There would be no rent. My only obligation was to do my best to keep the place up, such as it was.

I could live there as long as I wanted and could move out at any time, with or without the King's displeasure.

If I moved out, I was to inform the waiter at the Deck Bar, who introduced me to the place, and return the keys to him.

He told me I could move in just as soon as he found passage to New York, probably within the week.

I dated it and showed it to him. He immediately signed it with a flourish and returned it to me. I signed it and was about to copy the few conditions for him to keep. He motioned it away, saying that I keep the only copy somewhere safe. That was fine with him.

I had never rented a place with such a liberal lease. I momentarily thought how I could fix the place up and rent out rooms, making a little business out of it. Fine, but first I had to get my head wrapped right and send my publisher a new manuscript to stop his nagging for my next book.

He showed me to the door, in part muttering something to the king, in part excitedly telling me how much I would love being there. As I was about to leave, he concluded by telling me he would only take his clothes and some books with him. Everything else was mine to use as I pleased. He would send me a message at the Hotel Baia in Cascais where I was staying. He grabbed my hand and held it with an iron grip.

Looking deeply into my eyes and with the utmost seriousness, he told me not to worry about anything that might seem strange. At night there might be sounds and shadows from the abandoned rooms and hallways, but they were all explainable by old water pipes and dust blown up by the wind coming through all the imperfectly blocked windows.

If I had any concerns, I was to tell the waiter at the Deck Bar, and he would resolve it. After he moved out, I could collect all the keys from the same waiter.

I replied that I had no concerns at all and was excited to live there. This brought a smile to his face and a slightly more relaxed grip on my hand. I would do my best to straighten things up and return the garden to somewhere near its past glory. Perhaps I would get the swimming pool ready for summer. I so loved to swim. Meanwhile, I would return to my hotel in Cascais and wait for his good news. He shook my hand vigorously and bid me good luck and farewell.

CHAPTER TWO

Late afternoon five days later, I was sitting on my hotel room balcony lost in thought, watching the rain mix with the winter waves. A knock on my door interrupted my revery. The bellboy handed me a letter from the strange valet.

It read that I should pick up the keys at the Deck Bar from the English-speaking waiter. I could move in! I thanked him with a tip and hurriedly left to collect my keys.

After a brisk walk to the Cascais train station, I just managed to catch the next train to Lisboa. Two stations later, I arrived at Estoril. I crossed the street and was at the Deck Bar within twenty minutes from reading the letter. I found the waiter drying glass beer mugs in the back. He noticed me and motioned for me to sit at a table. I ordered a pint of one of the beers they brewed themselves.

He set the beer down in front of me. I showed him the letter and asked for the keys. He squatted down to be at my face level and whispered that the keeper of the palace gave him strict instructions to give me the keys only in the early morning and that I should return for coffee the next day at 0800.

"What difference could the time of day be?" I asked. He just shrugged his shoulders.

"This just makes no sense," I tried to remonstrate with him. "This is just wasting my time. Now I have to spend another night at the hotel." I tried to reason with him. Nothing worked.

Finally, he told me in a stern voice, "Look. You just have to believe that he had a good reason for it. I have no idea what that reason may be. All I can say is that I have known him for many years. He has an excellent sense of judgement. I trust him and so should you." With that weak non-explanation, he abruptly turned his back to me and strode to the back of the bar.

There was nothing else to do but finish my beer and return to Cascais. I chose to walk back along the Paredão. The walk would take about forty minutes. No sense to rush back with nothing to do but wait.

The winter waves were picking up, crashing on the rocks three meters (ten feet) below. Sometimes they would rise and splash my feet. My shoes were quickly soaked. But no matter, I loved the wild ocean waves and piercing winter wind. They spoke to my troubled soul, though I could not make out the words.

I thought of the hundreds of thousands who sank beneath the waves over the many millennia of seafaring time. Their souls moaning from their watery graves far below were barely audible over the shrieking wind and booming waves. Was it a simple collective groan of despair, or were they trying to communicate with me? If so, were they expecting an answer, or was it a warning?

Being a sensitive kind with a very fertile imagination, Nature had always communicated with me. Whether it was the wind, waves, birds, whatever, there was always a message in it. I just had to empty my mind and listen. But my mind would not be silent that cold late afternoon.

Alone on the wave swept path, there was nothing to distract me. I dropped the reins and let my mind wander to where it wanted. I started recalling the reason I was walking along that particular wet winter pathway. My mind returned to the exact place I was escaping from: my divorce.

On one of the wooden benches facing the ocean, I sat and pondered all the details of my broken dreams. I so dearly loved my ex-wife, but that love was never returned. She was the wealthy daughter of Russian emigres to New York via France.

She was super model beautiful with a bright charming personality, so unusual for her people. Unfortunately, she believed the world revolved around her and had no sense of morality. When we married, her father warned me that she was my problem now. That was only one of many red warning flags that I ignored, being blinded by a searing love.

My experience with her pains me still. I gave her everything and loved her with all my heart. If she thought she was the center of the universe, I tried to make it so. Despite all of that, she had a terrible temper and carried on with one of my closest friends for years. Even after the evidence was becoming dismayingly too obvious to ignore, I still wasted many more years floundering in the cesspool of self-denial.

One day I came home from a business trip a day early. I arrived home in the late afternoon, and she was not there. I was beside myself when I fell asleep alone. The next morning, I finally snapped and changed the door locks. It broke my heart, but I still had a shred of self-respect, enough to put an end to my abuse.

I wanted to continue in my self-absorbed misery when a wave crashed over me. The freezing winter water of the Atlantic drenched me, yanking me back to the present. I gathered my thoughts and squished my way back to the hotel.

After returning to the center of Cascais, I stopped in the little wine shop behind the hotel and bought an Alentejan wine for my room. After a hot shower, I sat on the little balcony high enough above the harbor as to escape the cloying, putrid stench. I opened the bottle and poured myself a glass, while I waited for room service to bring me one of my favorite Portuguese meals: baked duck and rice (arroz com pato). I watched the sun setting behind the Cascais lighthouse. Dark clouds were moving in for a stormy night.

Cascais Harbor from the Baia Hotel. Now the harbor smells fine
and the President of the Republic swims regularly in it.

Black clouds of the impending storm ushered in the night's darkness. I finished my wine and went inside, shutting out the chilly wind. I tried to write a few lines, but I kept thinking about the derelict palace that I would soon call my new home. So, I gave up and packed the few things I brought with me to start my new chapter in life.

Before turning off the lights, I read a dozen pages from one of Lovecraft's newly discovered stories. For reasons I could not explain, his bizarre, baroque horror tales calmed my restless spirit. But that night, the wind's high-pitched howl prevented me from falling asleep as soon as my head hit the pillow, as was normal for me.

Tossing and turning every ten minutes, I was about to reach for the ear plugs I use on planes. Suddenly, I heard someone speaking, but the wind was drowning out the words. I strained to hear.

It seemed to be speaking from my hotel's balcony. I listened carefully and then I realized it was not a voice buried by the wind, but the wind itself speaking. That realization made me feel better than the idea that someone was outside my room attempting to break in. To me, a speaking wind was always less threatening than a speaking person.

What was it trying to say? I could not make out any individual words. It reminded me of someone speaking in the next room separated by a wall, or even more accurately, someone speaking underwater. As I lay listening, sleep finally came.

I dreamt that I was flying on the winds of the storm, tossed about this way and that. Then I became the wind itself with the power to knock over trees and to flounder ships on the rough seas that I created. As the new day was gently tugging me into wakefulness, I resisted, preferring my dream world to the real one. Then I remembered that this was the day I would move into my new home.

That thought successfully made me stuff the winds back into their jinni bottle. The bedside clock indicated it was already 0700. There was only an hour until I could get my keys. I rushed through my morning ablutions, packed up, told the hotel to call me a taxi, and checked out. Before entering the taxi, I gave my new address to the concierge in case any letters came for me. I rode the ten minutes to the Deck Bar.

The rain had stopped, but it was still a wet, chilly morning. I told the taxi driver to wait for me, but he did not want to. So, I invited him to have breakfast with me. He accepted. We sat at a table by the window. My waiter came over and we ordered a simple Portuguese breakfast of coffee and a sweet roll.

I asked if he had something for me and he answered to meet him downstairs in a few minutes, where the restrooms were. I did so, and he gave me the keys. I asked what the big deal was about handing me the keys down there? He replied that he did not like to conduct private business in the public eye.

There were nearly thirty old, heavy, tarnished keys on a large iron ring that looked like what I imagined a dungeon keeper would have. He explained that one of them was a skeleton key, but I would have to find that one myself.

He told me that there were a few things I needed to know about living there. He explained to me the old water pipes and shadows at night. I told him I already heard all that before. But no, there was more. Before he could explain, his boss yelled down the stairs that new customers needed service. He told me to come back another day and he would explain the rest.

Shrugging my shoulders, I nodded that I would, though he never did, and followed him up the stairs. I finished my espresso and croissant while the taxi driver finished his cigarette. I paid the small bill and asked the waiter to explain to the taxi driver how to find my place. We left for the brief climb up the hill to my new palace home. After many one-way narrow streets, we arrived a few minutes later.

There it was. The big rusting green gate and the dreary moldering ruin that would be my home was just as I remembered it nearly a week before. The driver could not believe that was a place where anyone could possibly live. I assured him it was the very place.

He started to help me carry my bags up to the great wooden door. As soon as I opened the iron gate, he could see the place clearly. He refused to go any further. Obviously extremely nervous about being there, he dropped my bags, ran back to his taxi, and sped away.

Shaking my head at the silly superstitions of traditional cultures, I tried several keys until I found the one that opened the door. I left the front door open to get some fresh air in the place and found my way to my apartment door. It was unlocked.

I entered and turned on the wall switch. A pale light shone from a porcelain lamp on the dining table. The dozens of old cobwebs reminded me of the many laundry lines haphazardly stretching above the tenement alleys of old New York. The stale dust produced a sneezing fit.

The furniture was complete, as was most everything else. The old Romanian took little with him. I looked all around me and wondered how the old kook, who talked to long dead kings, could have lived in such a place. Even the windows were bricked up. I did not notice any of this the first time he showed me the place. My eyes must have been blinded during my first visit by a romantic's lenses.

The first thing I had to do was search the tool shed for a sledgehammer, which fortunately I discovered. I knocked out the bricks blocking up the window frames and let in the morning light. Fortunately, the windows still had their glass panes, and once closed, could keep out the cold air. I found cleaning supplies under the kitchen sink and spent the next four hours cleaning the dust and cobwebs. Now I understood why the waiter did not want me to move in at the day's dying light.

I inspected everything else. Nothing had been used in decades. Why did he not fix things? The electricity and gas worked. The water worked, but I had to let it flow for a few minutes to clear out the rust from the pipes.

The hot water did not work. After inspecting the water heater, I knew which parts I needed to replace the next day. Being a homeowner in the US forced me to be something of a handyman. I could take one cold shower if I had to.

I busied myself during the evening, washing all the bedding and towels. I made a list of other things I needed and prepared to go to bed. I was too tired to write anything, so I inspected the books left on the bookshelves. They were in every European language except English. I sighed and looked for the next best thing, books in French.

A book of Rimbaud's poetry in the original French would certainly put me to sleep. As I turned around, I was startled to see an old man standing in my living room, staring at me. Trying to hide my nervousness, I asked him who he was and what did he want.

He replied in a language I could not understand. He continued to speak for nearly five minutes straight, seemingly without even taking a breath, before he stopped. I apologized for not understanding anything and pointed to the door for him to leave. He spun around and returned into the darkness.

I sat down for a few minutes to stop my heart from racing. After gathering my thoughts, I realized that I had left the front door open to let in the air and had forgotten to close the gate when I first entered that morning. A drunkard had wandered in. I went out into the darkness and closed the gate and doors. I did not see him. Though he was not in the least threatening, I locked my apartment door securely, in case he returned with a changed mind.

Sitting on the bed with clammy hands and a beating heart, I realized how much the strange encounter shook me up. I had forgotten to buy any wine and had even forgotten to eat dinner. I was so busy. I had not thought of it. It was too late, so all I could do was turn off the lights and sleep my first night in the strange place I now called 'home'. I immediately fell into the deep sleep of the dead. Nothing could wake me.

CHAPTER THREE

The next morning, I rubbed the deep sleep from my eyes and pondered my strange dream. I was laying as a cadaver on a block of ice surrounded by many dark murmuring shadows studying me. I could neither understand their words nor see their faces. I shook off my dream and started the new day full of energy.

My plan was to spend the mornings fixing the place up and the afternoons writing my next novel. I felt newly inspired to write something wonderful in the eyes of the public. I started by cleaning my apartment and stocking up the kitchen with food from the local town market. Then I moved on towards the entrance, cleaning the impressive dining room next to my apartment, the two sitting rooms, the billiards room, and then the foyer.

In the afternoon. I would sit at my desk strangely inspired by the wildly overgrown ruin of a garden outside my window and tap out on my typewriter page after page, stopping only when the darkness signaled time for dinner. After dinner, I would walk the storm swept Paredão until I sat on one of the benches facing the winter Atlantic.

This was my solitary life. I was not lonely, as I lived in my characters who occupied my mind and spilled their lives on to my pages. The front part of the palace was clean and livable again.

The palace today, completely renovated.

I ignored the dark halls with their locked doors that disappeared beyond my rooms. I enjoyed the savage gardens surrounding me. They helped with my writing. The only thing I could complain of then was having the same strange dream every night.

Three weeks after I started this weird new chapter of my life, I entered the local post office to mail my finished manuscript to my publisher. It was a great relief, as this novel was a heavy burden that needed to be released into the world.

My novels were famous for the same dark mood, a cross between Lovecraft and Poe. This strange combination worked in the public's imagination. It seemed to capture the national angst of a new uncertain age in the post-Vietnam War and post-Watergate years. In my latest, I created a Dostoevsky-type main character, who describes his own slow descent into madness. I believe it will prove to be my best.

I had written nothing in six years and my publisher was beginning to lose hope that I would ever return to my former glory, although I gave him five New York Times bestsellers over the space of ten years. I guess my married life had drained all the creativity from my mind. The difficulties of dealing with my ex really were too much.

Leaving the post office lighter in spirit, I considered what to do while I waited for the response from my publisher. It was not yet the end of January, with two or more months of winter ahead. The grounds and swimming pool would have to wait until the rains stopped in the Spring.

That evening, I treated myself to a fine meal at one of the expensive restaurants surrounding the casino. I walked the Paredão as usual and went to bed late. Sometime around 0200, I awoke to shrieking sounds in the hallway and a great rattling of the walls. I ran into the hall and saw black wisps blowing through the air. Enraged at being awakened like that, I shouted to the moving shadows to stop the racket.

The shadows did immediately quiet down. I returned to my bed, resolved as my next project to close all the sources of the wind and give the place a complete dusting. I fell asleep marveling at my power to quiet the winds; something King Canute could not do to the rising tide. It was also the first night that I no longer dreamed of laying on a block of ice.

The next day, having discovered that I did not have keys to many other rooms, I needed to patch the walls from the outside. I found a ladder, wood, nails, and a hammer in the tool shed and started patching the holes that were allowing all the shrieking. As for the rattling water pipes, they would have to wait until I had more money.

After another good meal and my Paredão walk, I fell asleep to Rimbaud. Again around 0200 I was awakened not by shrieking and rattling in the hall, but from a great pounding on my ceiling from the rooms above me. I hate being awakened for any unnecessary reason.

Yet, someone in the room above me in a house where I had no neighbors was carrying on in the middle of the night. Angrily stomping up the stairs, I found the source of the racket. The old, thick door was locked tightly. I pounded on it, shouting for them to stop making noise so late at night.

They stopped, and everything was silent. I decided I had to make sure all the windows were securely blocked the next day to keep the drug addicts from using the place as a den of derelicts. I was quite dismayed when I found there was no obvious way into those rooms above me. I kept a crowbar under my bed that I found in the tool shed. If they returned, I would pry the door off the hinges and throw them out physically. But they never returned.

It was still hard to sleep. The shrieks turned into tortured moans. The rattling walls produced random knocks. I noticed everything calmed down after 0300 or 0400. I decided to change my daily routine to going to sleep then and waking up before noon. Being a writer allowed me to spend my days however I wanted.

I took up the Portuguese habit of eating late. After dinner ended at around 2300, I would sit at one of the bars in the casino until I had my fill. After that, I would spend the next few hours on the dark, empty Paredão, lost in the embrace of the wind and the waves.

It was on such a night that my life changed completely. That was when I met her. I was sitting on my favorite bench, lost in one of my strange profound daydreams, completely dazed by the bizarre events my mind was creating for me. My unconscious was bubbling up unfermented thoughts to my subconscious, which I could only reach in a trance like state.

While I was in my dream state, a woman in white appeared and offered her hand. I took it, and she led me to a garden of fragrant plants and flowers I had never seen. She undressed us both, and we entered a refreshing pool fed by a small waterfall trickling down from above us. The fragrance of the plants around us and the fresh, clear water that held my body were beyond anything I had ever imagined.

Her beauty was perfect. She embraced me, looked me in the eye, and led me to a soft grassy knoll shaded by strange leafy trees. She pulled me down onto her as she laid on the soft, warm grass. The passionate love we made was beyond my experience, limited as it was. As we were about to consummate our passionate union, my racing heart awoke me.

With my eyes still closed and my thoughts being gathered, I realized two things: if I were to fall into strange dreams on a seaside bench, it would be better to do so in the comfort of my bed and, also, I realized how lonely I was from years of an empty marriage. This painful emptiness made me live like a hermit in a foreign land for over a month.

But then, I felt a presence. Someone was sitting next to me. I turned and there was the same beautiful woman from my dream trance! Her face was even more radiant than in my dream. Not only was she very pale but also wore a diaphanous white robe that shone in the moonlight.

She was as astounding as I remembered her by the trickling pond moments before. But her eyes! It was her eyes that I could not make out before. They were cat's eye green that seemed to have a fire dancing behind them. They verily shimmered. I had never seen eyes like that. She was looking at me intently, almost quizzically.

She broke the silence. "I answered your call. I am here. Now what?"

I was dumbfounded and could not speak until I could collect my thoughts. Did I call her to join me? Called her through some bizarre magical process that made dreams come true? Or was she an odd local woman who enjoyed playing with lonely men's minds?

One look told me she was not a typical Portuguese. Her skin was almost a translucent white and her hair was a lighter shade of brownish red that reminded me of a certain animal's fur, an animal that I could not quite place. She was completely different from the cinnamon-colored local people.

She spoke English with a slight foreign accent that I could not place. Her voice was nearly a purr.

After I recovered enough sense, I answered her. "I didn't call you. I don't even know you or your phone number."

She looked at me with a demure smile. "You don't need a phone to call someone."

"Look, I don't know you, but you are welcome to share this bench with me."

"That would be good. You are very shy, aren't you?"

"Well, yes, I am shy. I guess that's why I'm a writer. I can create whole worlds filled with characters, who do and say exactly as I want."

"Ah, a writer? That does explain a lot."

"What does that explain?"

"It explains why you spend hours at night sitting on this bench listening to the waves and the wind. Also, why you dream much of the time like cats and dogs who prefer their dream life to their real one."

"Ah, so you are spying on me!" I was quickly becoming nervous, not sure what to do in this strange circumstance. My heart was beating like a kettle drum. Trying to regain a scrap of composure, I continued, "Look, it's getting very late. It's been a long day, and it's time to go home."

"Sure, I understand. It is indeed late. We'll continue our conversation tomorrow night. Same place and time?"

"Fine. We'll meet on this bench at the same time tomorrow." I rushed away, nearly running back to the safety of my palace. I was not at all sure if I was brave enough to see her again. I had a whole day to decide what I wanted to do.

CHAPTER FOUR

Back safely in bed, I was engrossed with my recent experience by the night sea. Those events so occupied me that I did not notice the occasional shrieks and rattling as the palace slowly calmed down to the quickly approaching day. I tried to get a hold of myself, though my mind was racing and my heart thumping against my chest.

Was I ready for a relationship so soon? Who or what was she, exactly? Maybe it was a good idea to have a new relationship to get over the nasty one I was escaping from. After an hour of staring at the ceiling, trying to calm my mind, I decided to put off all thoughts on the subject until the next day. The whole thing wore me out and I fell into a deep sleep, waking just before noon.

My dream was the same as the trancelike revelry I experienced on the bench before she sat down beside me. That seemed to indicate that I should meet her again, but then my logical mind took over. Doubts flooded back in. I determined that I would not decide anything and see what I would do at the appointed time.

Deciding that I would concentrate on writing to force me to think of something else, I sat in a local café the entire day. After many espressos, I had a late dinner at one of my favorite restaurants. After a bottle of Douro wine, I realized that I was putting off deciding what to do. So, I rose, paid my bill, and stepped outside.

I stood in front of the doorway for about five minutes with an empty mind, waiting to see what my feet would do. To my surprise, they chose to walk back home. Feet and mind agreed that, as intriguing as she was, things were just too strange. It was safer to stay alone.

Back in my living room, I tried to read. But the wine would not let me make any sense of it. So, I rose, took my flashlight, and wandered through the halls. I walked among the shrieking black dusty wisps and by the rasping rattling walls, ignoring them both. Lost in thought, I climbed the stairs to the second floor (or the first floor, as I learned that is what the Portuguese call it).

At the far end of the hall, one of the doors was open with a pale light spilling into the corridor. With wine-fortified courage, I quickened my pace to see who invaded my palace. I entered and at first noticed no one, marveling at the much better furnished and larger apartment than what I had. I thought that I should move into this far superior apartment the next day.

Then I noticed a man sitting at a desk writing a letter. He was the same one who accosted me the first night I moved in. He looked up and started another tirade in his unknown language, pointing to the door. I guessed he meant for me to leave. My indignation rising, I shouted back, also pointing to the door, that this place was mine and that he must leave now.

"Ah, you're American." He switched to the Queen's English. "Come, let's sit in the drawing room and discuss this situation."

I could not help but follow him to the elegantly appointed room where he motioned. I had fallen into his power of persuasion.

"It's too late for tea. How about some cognac?"

I nodded my agreement. He returned with two sniffers generously poured. Rage was again filling my heart at the idea that a homeless person was taking advantage of the small treasures of my home. But how did he learn to speak such perfect English, I wondered? I decided that being addicted to drugs ruins even the best educated.

"Now look here, my dear fellow, this is my home and has been far longer than since you moved in. How did you even find your way here in the first place?"

"No, you look here. The caretaker has rented this place, all of it to me alone. It doesn't include you. I have a signed lease to prove it. Shall I go and get it?"

"Don't bother. It doesn't matter, really. I know this man of whom you speak. He did not have the authority to make any decision regarding my home."

"Your home? Just who are you? Or should I ask, who do you think you are?" I demanded, becoming ever more aggravated.

"Never mind who I am. Who are you?"

"I am a famous American writer or was, anyway. I decided to change my environment to help inspire me to get my writing career back on track?"

"And you chose here?"

"Yes, because it fits into my state of mind. You see, I am trying to recover from a nasty divorce from a terrible marriage."

I could not help falling into the American habit of telling a complete stranger very personal things. Besides, he had an easy-going demeanor and a rich voice that simply mesmerized me. I decided that I should regain my high-horse and make him leave.

But then he commiserated, "Ah, a divorce. I understand completely. I, too, experienced a nasty divorce with a rich arrogant Greek woman. Unfortunately, we had a son who hates me now. Does the gentleman have any children?"

"Oh no, thank the gods!"

Our conversation ranged from general complaints about women by bitter men to the state of the world. We talked for an hour or so until every other sentence was peppered with a yawn.

He was fading faster than me. So, he concluded our impromptu meeting. "Fine. Look, it's getting very late, or should I say getting very early. I sense the day is quickly approaching. Let's discuss this

King Carol II of Romania in his better days (thanks to Wikipedia).

tomorrow. Meanwhile, feel free to stay here as long as you like. My palace is big enough for both of us."

"Your palace? You are very generous for a homeless man, probably a drug addict with an addled brain."

"Now, I don't want to get into a debate about it. Besides, my mind is shutting down and I need to sleep. Let's meet again tomorrow night."

Sleep beckoned me to my bed, too. The second glass of cognac was doing its work. I rose, bid him good night, and found my way back into the corridor. The door shut behind me, eliminating the weak light that showed my path back downstairs. With my flashlight's help, I retraced my steps through the now quiet halls, cleared of dusty dark wisps. The old, stale smell of a tomb still permeated the air.

In my bed, I resolved to return the next night and throw him out. I would bring a spade as a weapon if I had to do it by force. I was angry with myself for being so nice to him. But then I marveled at how charming he was, for that was the best word to describe him. Maybe I would let him stay there after all, but he would have to pay rent and part of the utilities. I flipped between being angry and being accommodating. Sometime after that, I fell asleep.

I awoke in the early afternoon. After my coffee and croissant in the salon with the magnificent marble fireplace, I went to see if he was awake. Perhaps he would like coffee and a croissant, too. Or maybe I will screw up my courage and toss him out.

The day light leaking through the cracks in the walls allowed me to find my way back upstairs easily. It was already ten hours after we spoke the night before. I knocked on the door, but there was no answer. Then I panicked a bit that I might not have been knocking on the correct door.

I knocked on all the doors on that floor, to no avail. I realized that I might not find his room again. Then a calming thought came that perhaps he was just a late sleeper, or, even better, that he moved out on his own accord. I decided to return at the same time I met him the previous night.

This strange man occupied my thoughts for the rest of the day. I distracted myself by going shopping at the local market. The smells, sights, and crowds distracted me for a few hours. I had another excellent Portuguese dinner, but with no wine. I needed a clear mind to deal with my odd squatting neighbor.

I returned to the second floor at the same hour of the night before. All the doors were shut. I pounded on the door I remembered. No answer. I pounded and shouted at all the doors on that floor. There were no answers or even sounds from any of them.

The bastard is hiding from me, I murmured to myself. I decided to return the next day with a sledgehammer and break down the door or all the doors if I had to. When I found him, I would throw him out. I was much bigger than him.

With this conclusion I fell asleep. The following day, after a breakfast of doubts, I worked up my resolve and found the sledgehammer in the tool shed. Returning to the second floor, again I knocked and shouted at all the doors. I resolved to force open all the locked doors in the entire palace. I should have done that right after I moved in. There was no reason to have any strange secrets lurking behind these locked doors.

Raising the sledgehammer, I struck the first door. The sledgehammer bounced back like I hit a piece of iron. The vibrations of the hit raced down the wooden handle and into my arms. I nearly dropped it on my feet. I swung again and again with the same effect. I tried the other doors with the same results. My arms were hurting badly so much I had to stop.

What were these doors made of? They looked and felt like wood, not the cold smoothness of metal. They did not even have a dent where I struck. I collapsed to the floor and pondered my situation. I clearly was not getting in through the doors. But what about the bricked-up windows? I could knock them out like I did with the bricks from the windows of my apartment.

I went outside and found the ladder. Judging what should be the correct windows, I climbed up armed with my heavy sledgehammer. I swung away with the same results of the night before, except this time it felt like I was pounding on the side of a rocky mountain. With one last heavy swing, I lost my balance and fell down into the bushes below. Clearly, I was not getting in that way either.

Lying on the cold wet ground, staring at the grey clouds forming wild foreboding shapes in the sky, I resigned myself to defeat. These rooms might as well be vaults in a bank or even sealed entrances to marble sepulchers. I had to accept him living there and decided that as long as he stayed out of my way, having another person living in that weird place might not be so bad after all.

I made a nice pizza in the grand oven of the kitchen beside the large dining room. A bottle of port wine of some age accompanied my dinner in the formal salon with a dining table that could sit twenty. I whiled away the rest of the evening in front of the fire I made in the enormous fireplace. The fire's crackling flames combined with the warmth of the port gently nudged me into slumber in my chair.

After the flames of the fire died down into embers, the damp cold of the dark night awoke me. I found my way back to bed. Sleeping soundly without my normal strange dreams, I felt refreshed the next day.

It was a good time to write at my favorite café with a view of the ocean. The ocean always both inspired and calmed me at the same time. And so, another day passed. As I was falling asleep that night, I realized I had not thought once about the strange woman in white for almost a week.

CHAPTER FIVE

The next day I puttered around the place, as my grandmother used to say, doing odd chores as I discovered them: fixed a rain leak here, oiled a rusty hinge there, etc. As the day's light turned into a pale dusk, I considered having an early dinner. The only restaurants where I could find that were in the casino, where they were open twenty-four hours a day.

The Chinese restaurant had reasonable dim sum. The only wine that goes with Chinese, or any Asian food, is a light semi-sweet white wine. So, I ordered a bottle of Vinho Verde from the very northern region of Minho.

The restaurant had a magnificent view that rolled past a wonderful water fountain down the slope of the dilapidated park to the little Estoril train station ending in the dark, heaving Atlantic. I dragged out the pleasant meal as long as I reasonably could. The pull of the Paredão was growing, and I felt a sense of dread about it.

Not wanting to see the source of this terrible attraction anymore, I removed myself to one of the casino's more attractive bars. Having no interest in the clanging, flashing slot machines or the depressing card tables, I found a bar away from all that. I was never a gambler. I always believed there was something wrong about trying to get something for nothing, every gambler's dream.

The view from Casino Estoril to the sea.

I sat down at the broad bar, a seat away from a richly dressed elderly man. Fortunately, he was in the mood for conversation. He asked me in French if I was Portuguese. I replied that I was not and if he wanted a meaningful conversation, we should speak English. He immediately changed to a slightly accented English. I always admired the polyglot multicultural Europeans. Our conversation proceeded like this:

"So, tell me. What brings a young American to these foreign shores?"

"'Young' is a relative term. I'm already forty-four. I came here to escape a personal tragedy. After the April 25 Revolution, Portugal has opened its doors to foreigners. It's the easiest place for us to acquire residency in Europe. What about you?"

"Me? I come here every year for the warm winters."

"I'm sure our Pennsylvania winters are even worse than yours."

"So they are. Did you know this casino was the inspiration for the Casino Royale book by Ian Fleming? Yes, he was a British spy stationed here during the Second World War. He stayed at the Palacio Hotel across the street.

"He and his fellows would play cards in the private rooms with their German counterparts, the Portuguese secret police, and other officials of Salazar's New State. The Portuguese loved being courted by both sides. It was a trade secret how to defeat your rival spies at cards but still let the Portuguese win. Poker was an essential skill in the spying business."

"No, I didn't know that."

"Yes, many of the James Bond films had parts filmed here in Portugal."

"Interesting. I'm a writer myself."

"Really? Tell me about it. What do you write? Have you been published?"

"Indeed, I have been published many times. Five of my books have been on the New York Times Bestseller list. I just finished one

Casino Estoril today.

and have already sent it to my publisher. I hope to hear from him any day now."

"What genre do you write?"

"Mainly horror, ghost stories, things like that."

"Hm, not really what I prefer to read."

"I never read the genre myself. It doesn't interest me personally. I must have a knack for telling a great story that can horrify others."

"What about you? Do you believe in ghosts and the spirits of the undead all around us?"

"Ghosts?" I laughed. "You must be joking! Of course not."

"How can you write convincingly about something you don't believe in yourself?"

"It's called 'imagination'. For example, I'm sure there are many priests who don't believe in what they preach. But they preach convincingly about the world unseen, about Holy Ghosts, for example.

"I grant you that. So, you don't believe in the spirit world? Perhaps you haven't experienced it yet. Or you have and you don't know it."

"Oh, give me a break! There is a scientific logical answer to everything, even if we don't know what that is due to our ignorance on the subject."

"Let me ask you this: How do you know I'm not a ghost, sitting here talking to you now? How do I know you're not a ghost?"

"Because I'm not."

"But that's exactly what a ghost would say, if asked."

"Come on! I see you holding your whiskey glass and drinking from it. I can grab your shoulder like this, and I feel something solid. That's how I know."

"How can you know anything on the subject, a subject that you don't even believe in its existence? How do you know that a spirit cannot appear as solid as a living person, doing the things a living person would do?"

"Because all the folklore about ghosts all say they are ephemeral. They can walk through walls, fly through the air, and the like."

"Is that what your ghosts do?"

"Yes, as a matter of fact they do."

"What about angels? Are they spirits?"

"I suppose they are, if they exist."

"If the Bible is anything to be believed, they do. And they are very solid. For example, Joshua wrestled with one. That angel spirit must have been very solid."

"That's just a Sunday School story."

"You're supposed to be the creative type with an imagination. Why would you not open your mind and believe in the very thing you write about? You expect your many thousands of readers to open their minds and believe that your story is real for at least the time they are reading it. I can tell you for a fact there are many millions of spirits roaming this world."

"For a fact? Really?"

"Absolutely. For example, do you see that well-dressed man with the beard over there wearing the old British officer's tunic full of medals and gold braid? The one playing at the roulette table?"

"Yes. He looks ridiculous."

"That's King George V of Britain, dead now over forty years. You must admit he's looking quite good, all things considered. Now, look over there. You notice the woman with the long faded pink dress dragging on the ground wearing the tiara? She's Maria Amelia, the last Queen of Portugal. Died twenty-five years ago at the age of eighty-six, but she looks like she was on the day she married King Carlos at age twenty. Quite radiant, isn't she? She was French, you know?"

"Now you're being ridiculous."

"Oh, quite the contrary, my dear sir. I'll continue. Next to her is her son, Luis Filipe, the crown prince who together with his father, King Carlos, was assassinated on the Praça do Comércio in Lisboa in 1908.

"On the other side of the casino, in his Russian navy uniform, is Grand Duke Alexander Mikhailovich, the brother-in-law of Tsar Nicholas II. Dead for forty-five years. Talking to him energetically is…"

"They all just came from a costume party. OK. I'll play along. How can you tell the difference between spirits and the living?"

"That's easy. All spirits have a faint glow around them. Do you see them?"

"You're being absurd and I…"

"Oh, and now just entering the casino is another one. I can tell by his glow. That looks like…" He suddenly turned away. His face became very white. He gulped down his whisky and went silent.

Peering across the crowded room, the elegantly dressed elderly gentleman looked very much like the strange one living in my palace. I decided to go find him after my conversation with the very odd man next to me.

He had recovered his composure and lit up a cigar. Puffing on it, he continued. "Enough of ghosts. Let's change the subject. So, where are you staying now? In one of the hotels?"

"No, I managed to get a great lease for an old manor house nearby."

"Really? Which one?"

"It's the former palace of a Romanian king, who lived here in exile, until he died in 1953."

"No! You don't mean that old bricked up wreck on the corner of Rua de Algarve and Rua de Alentejo?"

"Yes, that's the one. There really is only one livable set of rooms, well, maybe two. It appears that someone else is living there. His rooms are much nicer and bigger than mine."

"Someone else is living there? Really? I bet I can guess who, but we decided to change the subject."

"It's possible you know him. Seems to me he just entered the casino. I've met him and have even been inside his apartment."

"Let's put it this way. The locals believe that place is haunted by the dead Romanian king. You'll never get me in there."

"Ah, now I know you aren't a spirit. A spirit would never be afraid of other spirits."

"How would you know that? How do you know there isn't a hierarchy of spirits? Or spirits which are good and others evil? Powerful evil spirits, angels of darkness, that could cast the good ones from this plane of existence to a hell where there is nothing but wailing and the gnashing of teeth?"

The Frenchman was clearly getting worked up. "There are angels, spirits of the God of Light and there are angels, spirits of the God of Darkness. Then there are the spirits of everyone else who happen to be in between."

"That is a fairy tale of old religions who want to cast their control over the minds of their believers."

"Ah, but I believed the same when I was your age. But trust me. I have far more age than you. Far more experience with both life and death. Yes, both life and death!" He was standing, towering over me, breathing heavily.

"Hey, calm down! Clearly, I don't know one way or the other. I'll give you the benefit of the doubt until proven otherwise. I think we need another round."

He sat down in silence and motioned for the bar tender to refill our glasses. I took this opportunity to consider how I could gracefully leave this strange and obviously drunken old man. I looked around my surroundings with slight hope that I may find someone else to talk to. Then I saw her!

The strange woman who caught my interest on the bench that night seemingly ages ago was hurrying through the lounge. She walked purposefully with the same white robes flowing behind her.

"Watch my drink! I just saw someone I need to speak with." I jumped up and rushed after her with all the same nervous tension from the night we met on that cold, wet bench. Until then, I had been so relieved to be rid of her memory. But now, not only was my mind tense and nervous, it was also full of the desire for her that I had tried so hard to deny. I thought I was happy in my solitary loneliness. Clearly, I was wrong as I hurried after her.

I almost caught up with her, but she disappeared into the women's restroom. Stopping before the entrance, I considered if I should go in after her. Would she be offended and not want to meet me again? I could not risk that. At that moment, another woman walked out of the restroom.

I asked her urgently, "Is there a woman in white in there? I need to talk with her!"

She looked at me with growing fear, indicating that I was being too aggressive in my questioning. "No. There was no one in there but me."

"But I just saw her enter! I must talk with her!" I started to open the door.

She blocked my path. "If you go in, I will call out to those two security men over there."

Yes, sure enough, there were two security men looking at us with some interest. I had no choice but to go sit on the leather seat across the hall by the men's room door and wait for her to come out. I was fuming over why that woman would lie to me about her not being in there. Perhaps she was protecting the woman in white from what she perceived to be a madman.

Impatiently waiting for about ten minutes, I was beside myself I might have lost her. My heart leapt when I saw her come out and quickly make her way to the casino exit. I ran after her, avoiding all the patrons who seemed to take delight in blocking my way. She was already outside. I ran out the door and just as I was about to catch hold of her, two security men grabbed my arms.

"Where do you think you're going?"

"That woman! I need to talk to her!"

"No, sir. You are not going anywhere until you pay your bar bill."

"Damn it! She's getting away!" She disappeared into the darkness with only the slight paleness of her robes shining through the fog.

"Pay your bill and you can chase after whomever you want. We don't want to ban you from the casino, but we will."

Seething with anger, I realized I had no choice but to return to the bar and pay my bill. I shook off their arms and reentered the casino. The two security men were right behind me. I stormed back to the bar. The old man was not there. The bartender was surprised to see us.

"Here he is. Back to pay his bill."

"Oh, sorry about that. False alarm. Another patron paid for him and left."

"We are terribly sorry, sir. Forgive us. We are just doing our jobs. Have a good time at the casino and hope to see you again soon. Here's a 500 Escudo voucher for the inconvenience. You can use it anywhere in the casino."

They turned and left me standing there shaking in impotent fury. I was about to tear up their voucher and throw the pieces back at them when I realized it was worth USD125, enough to eat and drink in the casino for months without paying.

My head now somewhat clear, I stuffed it in my pocket, calmly exited the casino door, and walked home. The whole scene both infuriated and shocked me by how quickly my mind turned from calm to complete turmoil. I had thought that I was 'over' her, though over what exactly, I could not say. Clearly there was a part of my mind that was still clinging to her memory, a part certainly irrational that took complete control of me.

It was close to 0300 when I returned to my apartment. I could not sleep as I stared into the darkness, pondering the bizarre conversation I had and then the whole scene of the strange woman in white. I was completely at a loss about what to do about her, or more importantly, what to do about me.

Early daylight was slipping through the cracks in the windows when I finally fell asleep. I dreamt of chasing after the alluring woman in white, never quite catching up to her like I was running through waist-high water. Her bare backside swayed enticingly just out of reach, but again her face was always hidden.

CHAPTER SIX

Dazed and exhausted from a sleepless night, I made a fire and sunk in the stuffed chair before it with my coffee and day-old croissant. All I could see in the dancing flames was her, the woman in white. My mind was in turmoil. I was shocked how quickly I fell apart at the casino the previous night.

I thought I was over her. Our brief strange encounter was already in the past, and I was safely alone again. She had a strange power over me, and that meant she was dangerous.

On the other hand, I could not stop thinking about her. Was she the same woman I dreamed of while staring at the heaving sea that night and created her out of my mind? Clearly, she was real, but did I summon her somehow? Could she pick up on my most personal thoughts?

Yet she did come and sat down beside me. She appeared to have an interest in me, but why did she escape so fast from the casino the previous night? Surely, she must have known I was trying to catch up to her.

The fire gave one last crackle and woke me up many hours later, just as the light grey of the afternoon was slipping into darkness. I dreamed that I was running after her, again waist high in water, barely able to move forward. After a long, slogging struggle, she finally stopped and turned to me.

Her face radiant, her wet robe revealing her powerfully attractive curves. She opened her arms and took me into her embrace. She pulled me down onto the beach and my heart was pounding like a fire alarm. Just as a powerful ecstasy was filling my entire being, the fire's crackle sent her falling away from me, disappearing into a sudden sinkhole of my mind.

I cursed the fire for tearing her from me. But the cold darkness of that crumbling salon brought me back to my senses. Ah, it was just a dream. My disappointment rapidly turned to excitement when I resolved to stop my silly indecision and return to that dark, frigid bench that now seemed so warm and inviting. Surely, she would return, and we can start whatever it was that I had stopped. It made no sense to my logical mind, yet it was as real as an edifice of granite in a public park.

It was raining when I finally was ready to face the night of either disappointment or culmination. I tried to have a long relaxing dinner at one of the casino restaurants, but I was just too nervous with anticipation. Even a bottle of Alentejo wine could not calm me. When I could no longer stand waiting, I paid and left.

Passing the wood-paneled bar from the previous night, I saw the same strange man ensconced on his stool from the night before. He saw me and gave me a thumbs up with a wink. I gave him a thumbs up back. Then I immediately wondered what he meant by it. It felt to me like he knew what my mission was that night and was wishing me good luck.

Back into the drizzle, I walked down the great green space that was the park rolling down to the Marginal, the main coastal road from Lisboa. Before I passed through the tunnel under the train station and finally to the esplanade along the sea, I had to walk past the Deck Bar.

My favorite Portuguese waiter stopped me. He beckoned me inside, out of the rain. They had received a telegram from the US addressed to me. I ordered a glass of their house wine and sat down to read it. It was from my publisher in New York. I did not remember giving the Deck Bar as my address, but it was clearly addressed to me at the Deck Bar of Estoril.

It read: **Just finished your manuscript Stop We have another NYT bestseller Stop We will wire you an advance of USD100,000 Stop Yes you read that right Stop Send bank details Stop Expect you will make USD500,000 in the first year Stop Congratulations Stop Keep writing Stop**

I wrote that book in just a few weeks after I arrived. The place, as strange as it was, obviously inspired me. I was dumbfounded. That was one of the biggest advances ever to any writer. If I returned to the US now, I would have been feted with interviews on TV and radio, invited to all the great literary societies, and busy with other promotional events like book signings, etc.

My imagination and storytelling ability had returned. I had money, a lot of it. I also knew that my next book would be at least as good, maybe better. I was on a roll, as they say. My life suddenly changed. I had written bestsellers before, but that was many years ago, before my marriage drained me like a water bug slowly sucking the life out of a frog caught in its claws.

Suddenly, options presented themselves. I could return as a famous celebrated author to the US, buy a nice place on the California coast, find a young jet set woman, and lead a fun life. No, I was not ready for that yet. At least I could move to a Portuguese palace that was fixed up and modernized. A place where there were no strangers living upstairs, and the night did not shriek and rattle. I considered that vision for a while and then I rejected that, too. My place provided creative inspiration and there was no price for that. Maybe after my next book, I would reconsider.

The telegram did do something unexpected. It removed the ominous foreboding of my hoped-for meeting with the strange woman on the Paredão. I found my stride again. I had money. Most importantly, I had my self-confidence. I did not need to meet anyone that was causing such an effect on me. In fact, I could just return home and forget about it.

My sensitive heart came to the rescue and reminded me that my heart was broken into splinters from an abusive, nasty marriage. I had a duty to myself to make me whole again. The best way to make someone in my situation whole again was to find a new relationship. That relationship may not, probably would not, last long. But at least, she, whoever she was, would make me forget the past and help me focus on the future.

Besides, I did not really need her. What is wrong with a successful, available, healthy man like me having some fun, anyway? After all that I had been through, I deserved it. Those were my thoughts as I continued my way through the tunnel to the Paredão on the other side.

The tunnel served as a frame for a moving painting of the restless winter waves. The streetlights splashed a pale light onto the esplanade but had no effect on the dark sea, with dangerous rocks appearing and disappearing as the waves crashed over them. Invigorated, I walked the ten minutes to my favorite bench and our meeting place. All my doubts were replaced with confidence. There was a spring in my step as I thought about my new exciting foreign adventure.

Ah, there was my bench, but it was empty. I refused to be disappointed. There would be no way that she would arrive before me. She was probably standing on the cliffs above, waiting for me somewhere warm and dry. I even looked up, expecting to see her waving at me. I could not make out any such place in the darkness.

I settled in to wait, well equipped for the cold, rainy winter night. I was dressed warmly with my foul weather gear. A wave could crash on top of me, and it would have no effect. What I was not prepared for was a long wait. I fully expected her to, if not waiting for me on the bench, at least be rushing up to me within minutes, apologizing for being late.

After thirty minutes of waiting and no one contritely apologizing to me, I considered how childish I was being. We had made a date for the next day at the same time, but it was me who never showed

The view from the bench.

up. As I remembered it, I had rushed off in a schoolboy panic. What kind of impression did I make by doing that? After considering it all, I concluded she knew I was trying to catch up with her the past night but did all she could to avoid me. She quite clearly ran away from me!

That thought threw my mind into turmoil. What was I thinking? Whatever gave me the idea that she was even interested in me? Was it my stupid manly ego kicking in, thinking that all women are secretly yearning for me? They just don't know it yet?

I was not doing so well, actually. All the excitement of my telegram had dissipated, replaced by anxiety buoyed by the swelling frustration and fear that she would never come. I tried to wrap my mind around that. It probably was best in the long run, all things considered. I should not really be getting involved with anyone now. After all, I reasoned, I had another bestseller to write.

I looked at my watch. I was waiting for an hour already. All my thoughts turned to anger. I was angry at her for not showing up, getting me all hot and bothered over nothing. I was angry at myself for inventing something that did not exist and getting seriously worked up by it. What really made me mad was that I had successfully removed her from my conscience and if she had never appeared at the casino, I would be having a strange but diverting conversation at the casino bar even then.

Staring out at the angry sea, I cleared my mind and calmed my pitching heart with a highly effective method of meditation. I closed my eyes and emptied my mind. I concentrated on my breathing, the soft movement of my breath flowing past my nostrils. It was working. But soon she appeared like in my dream of the previous night. I fought her image by concentrating again on my breathing. But she managed to pull me back to her.

My mind fought back and forth like that for maybe twenty minutes. I gave up and warm myself at the bar with that odd acquaintance. Besides, I still owed him for the night before. A few drams of whiskey would distract me, reminding me of what is really important. That is just what I needed. It was time to stop this nonsense.

I stopped my struggle, opened my eyes, and rose to leave. There she was, sitting by my side, staring at me the whole time I was trying to meditate her out of my mind. I fell back onto the bench and missed, falling to the hard, wet pavement below. In my embarrassment I recovered my seat but had still not found my voice. I was so shocked I was speechless.

"Did you call?" she asked in her sulky, sexy, deep voice exactly as she asked the first time we met. I opened my mouth to answer but could not form any words.

"Hello? I answered your call. Here I am. Now what?"

CHAPTER SEVEN

"Now what?" was exactly the question that echoed in my mind. As I was trying to process the fact of her presence and the implications of that question, she stared expectantly into my eyes with her orbs of green fire. She repeated her question in her low, sultry voice.

Controlling my panic, I managed to blurt out, "It's you! You're here!"

"Yes, I'm here. Care to answer my question?"

"I don't know. I mean... now what? I guess now we have a pleasant conversation."

"OK. You start."

"Start? Um, fine. How did you know I was here? How did you find me?"

"Like I always do. You called me here."

"Not this again. I did not call you. I have no phone and I don't know your phone number even if I did."

"Now you're being silly. I heard your call as clearly as I hear the waves crashing below us now. And I came. Do you want me to go?"

"No, no, no, please stay a while. I mean, I guess I've been thinking about you a lot lately. I was thinking about you even now."

"Well, there you go. You called me just like I said."

"That can only mean you can receive my thoughts, like a mind reader. That you can read my thoughts from a distance. How can that be?"

"Look, your heart called out to me, and I answered. If we can't get past this, we're wasting our time. I hate wasting time. Can we talk about something else, or should I leave?"

"Fine, fine, never mind. Yes. Let's change the subject. You know, I saw you at the casino last night. I tried to catch up with you, but you were in such a hurry to leave."

"At the casino, did you say? I don't remember that."

"You don't remember where you were last night?"

"I don't remember seeing you last night. Besides, I hate gambling."

"I agree. Seems to me something is not right about trying to get something for nothing. And losing so much trying to do so."

"So, why would I go to the casino?"

"For the same reason I do, to have a decent meal."

"That's a reason I can accept. You told me you've been thinking about me for a while now, yet I haven't seen you on your favorite bench by the sea. I haven't heard you calling for me, either."

"Calling for you? Don't know. Maybe I've been avoiding you because I am a bit frightened of you."

"Frightened of me? Do you think I'm some kind of spirit, a ghost, a phantom?"

"Even if you were, I wouldn't be afraid of you for that reason. I'm not afraid of ghosts. I don't even believe they exist, though I write about them in my books."

"You write about matters that you believe don't exist? How can you write about things you know nothing about? Don't even believe in?"

"Now if you want to put doubts into my head about the one thing I can do well, I believe it would be better to end whatever it is we have started right now." I was getting annoyed by strangers questioning my writing abilities. I grabbed the telegram in my pocket instinctively as a shaman would his talisman.

"Fine, whatever. Believe or don't believe in whatever you want. It's not important, anyway."

"It's not important for what?" I asked defensively.

"Look, I didn't come here to discuss the meaning of life. I also don't believe that's why you want me here with you. So, why is it that your heart calls for me? Think before you answer."

I went silent for a few minutes, pondering her question. When she occupied my thoughts, it was always something physical, sexual, in fact. Was it that simple? If I wanted sex, there were any number of willing women hanging out at the casino. No, it must be more than that. If so, what was it?

There indeed was something else. She was mysterious, a complete enigma to me. She intrigued something deep inside me as if she were awakening a secret unknown power or spirit within me. Something else besides my loins was stirring to life.

Or was it as mundane as trying to find someone only to distract me from my painful memories? Even if it was as simple as that, there was nothing wrong with it. I mean, we are all adults with free will.

I stopped myself when I remembered she could probably understand everything that was percolating in my head. So, I stopped thinking and just threw out the first answer that came to mind.

"Because I'm lonely, I guess. You're also incredibly attractive to me. I won't bore you with the reasons I came to Portugal except to say it had something to do with a seriously broken heart."

"Well, my dear, we can't have you passing your days, years perhaps, with a broken heart, can we? What can I do to help?"

"What can you do to help?" Immediately, I pictured laying with her, melting into her, on that beach of my dream. I could not help it. As soon as I did, she understood. Playing for time, I asked rhetorically, "How do you think you can help?"

"Oh, I'm sure I know just the method. Tell you what. You're getting cold and it's getting late. Why don't you come over to my place tomorrow night for dinner?"

My heart nearly leapt from my chest. That was precisely what that strange and fickle organ wanted to hear. "Ah, that would be great! Yes, I would love that very much. Where and what time? Should I bring anything?"

"Only bring your good self. I'll write my address on this scrap of paper. Don't lose it. You already know that we southern Europeans eat late, well after the sun sets. Come by around ten. Would that be fine?"

"Fine? Yes, that would be wonderful!" I looked at the address to confirm it. I could find it. I knew the street. I could walk there in less than ten minutes from my gate.

Suddenly, a surge of electrical heat flushed through my entire being. This was exactly what I had been yearning for, despite being in self-denial about it for weeks. She clearly wanted me, or at least was interested in me. My part was to make her desire me, no, to need me.

"Hello? I'm still here, you know."

I did not realize I had shut my eyes and went silent with her still sitting next to me. "Sorry. I was merely thinking…"

"I know what you were thinking. Don't fret about it or over think it. Just come by tomorrow night. Let's see where this takes us. In the meantime, it's time to get some sleep. Don't you agree?"

"OK, don't overthink it." I repeated. "Fine. I'll see you tomorrow night. Should I walk you home?"

"Don't be ridiculous. Besides, I have my driver waiting. See you tomorrow. Make sure you come with a strong appetite." She squeezed my thigh and kissed me lightly on the cheek.

Before I could reach for her and kiss her in return, she was already on her feet and walking away. I leaned back on the bench and stared at the cloudy, starless sky, not seeing anything. I wondered for at least half an hour what just happened. My mind was tumbling with random thoughts, all desirable.

What a day it was! First, the wonderful telegram that put my professional, not to mention my financial life back on track. Then there was this very strange turn of events with this mysterious but infinitely desirable woman just inviting me to dinner and likely more the very next night. This could put my personal life back together again. If so, then I would be on my feet again in every way. My next follow-up novel could be only a few weeks away.

After a wave nearly drenched me, I forced myself off the bench and walked my solitary path back home. The only thing I needed to do at that point was to stay healthy. The last thing I wanted was to come down with a cold. That would stop this budding relationship in its tracks.

I stopped and asked the empty space around me: *Did I just say to myself 'relationship'?* I answered myself with a murmur that I was starting to overthink it, something she told me not to do. That would be hard for someone like me, who lives in my mind all the time, constantly overthinking everything.

All the little restaurants and cafes were already closed. The casino was still open, with its neon lights flashing like a beacon, attracting the lonely moths to its shores. I steered myself away and up the hill to the strange derelict palace I called home.

It started to rain as I placed the heavy key into the front gate. The creak of the hinges reminded me that I needed to oil them the next day. By the time I walked up to the columned portico above the front door, it opened for me. My strange upstairs neighbor was standing above the stairs to the entrance holding up an antique oil lamp. He looked rather cross with me.

He stepped aside to let me enter. "Out very late tonight, are we?"

"Are we? I guess we both are. Are you going somewhere now?"

"No, I was simply waiting. I was a little worried. Wanted to make sure we were alright."

"Sorry, I should have called to put your mind at ease. But I didn't pass any payphones. Do you even have a phone?"

"Sounds like someone is being sarcastic. We are not being sarcastic, are we?" His voice took on a weird air of menace. I really did not want to be on anything but the best terms with this strange man.

"No, no, nothing like that. If you must know, I was meeting a friend."

"Yes, I know. Are we not moving too quickly with someone with whom we are barely acquainted? Already calling her a 'friend', are we?"

"Well, maybe a friend is a strong word."

"It sure is, especially since we know nothing about her."

"How do you have any idea what I know or not know about her?"

"We know nothing about her, not a thing. Yet, we are practically head over heels in love with her. What do we know? Hm? Do we even know her name? Well, do we? Tell me, what's her name?" His voice became shrill and filled the darkness beyond his feeble lantern. His question echoed in my ears.

"OK, you're right. Don't get worked up over it. You're not my mother giving me the first degree for coming home late." I could not hide my annoyance with this strange, interfering man. I was also annoyed that he was right.

So, I answered his question. "You're right. I know nothing about her. But so what? I do know she is an extremely attractive woman. That is enough for now. I am a man, and she is a woman. We are attracted to each other. What's more important than that?"

"There is plenty that is important. A moth doesn't know the name of the flame that so attracts it. Be careful with our obsession. I fear we are entering dangerous waters, extremely dangerous waters. Now good night. I must return to my rooms. The dawn is coming soon, and I need to sleep." And he turned to leave.

I stood watching his little hunched form with his little light disappearing down the long hallway. My head was spinning with another strange, even unpleasant experience, the first one of the day. But it was a day almost ended. I needed a hot shower and a heavy blanket.

Later, as I huddled in my bed, I stared into the darkness. Sleep was dimming my mind like a clock slowly winding down. Yet one question remained. Out loud, I asked the four silent walls around me, "*What is her name?*"

CHAPTER EIGHT

Just before noon the next day, I awoke to the birds chirping in the trees sheltering from intermittent bouts of rain. It took several moments before my thoughts could focus. Then I remembered. Today was the day! The day we would finally meet at her place to spend some quality time together. I was suddenly as excited and agitated like Christmas morning when I was eight years old.

Halfway through my rushed breakfast, I stopped myself. There was no sense to rush through anything, as I still had nearly ten hours to wait. So, I stopped wolfing down my simple breakfast and coffee. I considered that if things go as planned, I should spend the night with her. That thought had been at the root of my fascination for her. It was nearly an obsession.

Realizing that it was really all about sex made it better for me. After some time of fun and we had our fill of each other, we could part ways amicably. My life would be tranquil again until the next one entered my life. The knowledge that I was in control of the situation eased my nervousness.

Thinking back on my marriage, I remembered the physical side. Which in fact was really the only thing we had, except my paying for everything and putting her on a pedestal. We started with great sex four and even five times a day. Towards the end it was only twice a year, on our birthdays, then only on my birthday. She figured thirty minutes a year was payment enough for the great life and security I gave her, which included the security of being able to take on other lovers.

I was reminded of a funny story my Cajun friend, Pierre, told me once about his first marriage. When he first met his wife-to-be, it only took a one-dollar bottle of wine to make love with her. Later, after they married and had two kids, it required a romantic dinner at an expensive restaurant, about fifty dollars. Eventually, it was about once a year, when he was paying a mortgage and everything else for about 100,000 dollars a year. It was about then that he figured he was literally paying 100,000 dollars to have sex once a year, while being heavily in debt with someone he was only in the habit of being with.

He did the math and told me that he could have had a hooker every three or four days for a hundred dollars a throw and still be ahead. While he was pondering that profound realization, a neighbor called him at work and told him there was a fire truck parked outside his house. Maybe his house was on fire?

He raced home and sure enough, there was indeed a fire truck parked in front of his house. He rushed in and was shocked to not find a fire, but his wife and her bimbo friend having a wild orgy with the local fire department. The first thought he had was why were all the men only wearing their fire helmets?

The next thought that came in his head was to ask her, "Where are the kids?" His wife calmly answered, "Don't worry. They're still at school." "Don't worry" was her answer!

The divorce and the child support cost him dearly. He decided having a hooker once a week was far safer, cheaper, and, better yet, it was a different woman every time. He could even splurge and have two on his birthday. He preferred the services of struggling actresses. At least they could act. He was poor, but he was happy.

I always chuckled when I remembered Pierre's story, until I inevitably considered the parallels with my own life, which brought dark thoughts into my heart, dark thoughts indeed. After considering all of that, I would quickly congratulate myself on being so self-controlled and clear-minded.

While going through my never-ending nasty divorce, a motorcycle buddy offered me a simple, almost elegant solution. He knew members of his motorcycle club, who for 500 dollars would take her on a one-way trip to the New Jersey pine barrens. Problem solved. I can happily report that despite serious consideration, I refused his kind offer. She was not worth the aggravation of being a prime suspect in her murder.

Considering that line of thought had run its course and still, with many hours to go, I decided to find something to fix up around the place with the few hours of sunlight left. That took my mind off everything but the job at hand until I could not see very well what I was hammering. Now what to do?

I ate petiscos, savory Portuguese café snacks I had come to enjoy, at a nearby restaurant until I was tired of sitting. Besides, I had to keep space for the special dinner later that night. With hours still to go, I walked aimlessly around the blocks of the neighborhood to pass the time, until I reminded myself that I needed to save my energy. I stopped at a bar to watch a football (soccer) game and drank some wine. Then I realized that I should not drink much before my date as that never helps anything.

In short, I had almost run out of options. I decided that I would go back to my apartment and take a nap. There could be nothing wrong with that. I set the alarm and fell into a restless, dreamless semi-slumber.

The alarm rang, and I shot out of bed as if I were probed with an electric cattle prod. Nervousness and excitement in equal measure took hold of me. I thought how we needed to have sex quickly so we can move out of this preliminary period of uncertain anxiety and into something calmer and surer, as sure as anything like a relationship can be. Maybe it was a delusional sureness, but I would be happy with that.

By the time I hurriedly slammed the gate behind me, I still had forty-five minutes before our fateful meeting. During the seemingly endless ten minutes it took to arrive at her street, I walked through a thick fog. The few working streetlights only emitted a pallid glow that did nothing to illuminate the dark wet streets.

The cold, damp air made me pull my coat tighter around me. The weather seemed to be telling me there was no good reason to leave the warmth of one's home on such a night. To emphasize the point, it started to rain.

I found the address she gave me. It was a derelict manor house on a smaller scale than the one I was living in. Even worse, there were no lights on inside. My anxious mind quickly turned to panic. Was it all one big joke? Was she playing with me like a cat with a mouse? I was clearly becoming infatuated.

Though I memorized her address, just to confirm, I reached into my coat pocket for the scrap of paper she handed me the night before. But it was nowhere to be found! How could I have lost such an important document? That scrap was as important to me as my publisher's telegram, which I luckily still could feel where I left it in my right coat pocket.

Just around the corner and out of sight of her house was a bus shelter. I sat down out of the rain and tried to get a hold of myself. My first ray of hope was that I was a half an hour early. Perhaps she was out and had not returned yet. I decided to wait not only the remaining thirty minutes, but maybe another thirty minutes, or even an hour, in case she was late returning home.

As for the address, I was sure I remembered it correctly. There could be no doubt of that. And besides, if things did not work out that night, I guessed we could meet again on that bench by the sea, if she had any interest. If she was not genuinely interested, then it was probably better in the end that I knew earlier than later. But I

One of her ruined houses 45 years later.

knew that was not really true. One moment with her would make it all worth it, no matter how long it lasted.

A bus came by and stopped, but I waved it away. The bus driver looked at me doubtfully, as if giving me time to reconsider. It was going to Cascais. I considered boarding it and finding bars in Cascais where I would get drunk to blot her out of my mind. The thought crossed my mind for an instant, but I waved him away again with unnecessary annoyance.

After looking at my watch every few minutes and forcing myself to stay calm, the time arrived. I jumped up and walked around the corner and up to her front gate. There were still no lights on. I opened the rusty, creaking gate and knocked on the door. I knocked and knocked, but no answer. I turned the doorknob. It was unlocked. But I stopped myself from entering. If she did not answer, she clearly was not ready for me yet. She might be angry to find me in her home uninvited. So, I retreated slowly back to my bus stop.

Somehow, I got through another thirty minutes of waiting, looking at my watch every minute or so. The wind was picking up and the cold damp air was getting to me. I returned to her forbiddingly dark, decrepit house. Again, I knocked on the door with no answer. Back at the bus shelter, my anxious impatience was turning into anger. The last time I waited on a cold forlorn street corner for a woman who never showed up was when I was in my early twenties.

I reasoned with myself that I did arrive half an hour early and that she really was 'only' half an hour late. I closed my eyes, trying to rein in my galloping mind, and concentrated on the plot of my next novel. But my plot constantly ended up with her. I would try a different path and again it would lead to her. I must have nodded off, as my thoughts were going nowhere and were exhausting me.

When I opened my eyes and looked at my watch it was already 2300, an hour after we agreed to meet. I resolved to check one more time and if she still was not there, I would go home and force myself to forget about the whole thing. I would avoid thinking about her and never return to my favorite bench facing the sea ever again.

I turned the corner and could not believe my eyes! There were lights on inside, weak lights, but signs of life, nonetheless. At once, my mental funk was replaced by euphoric hope. My mind rebounded from near despair to joy, with no trace of the anger that filled my heart just a short while before.

The gate creaked open with a loud squeal that must have woken up the neighbors of the entire block. As I approached the door, it opened and there she stood, all in white as usual. I saw lines of candles flickering behind her.

"Here you are! I was starting to think that you changed your mind, or even worse, forgot about me."

"Me? Oh, no, not at all. I've been waiting at the bus shelter around the corner since 2130. I came by a few times since and everything was dark. I thought you were the one who forgot about me."

"2130? No one comes early to a soiree in Europe, my dear. And nothing starts on time. You must expect everything to start at least forty-five minutes or even an hour later than the time spoken. Why, we would consider it rude if someone arrived early. I see a storm brewing. Well, don't just stand there. Come in."

She smiled alluringly, and all was right in my world again.

CHAPTER NINE

Come in, she said, I'll give you shelter from the storm echoed through my head from the old Dylan song as I entered. She took my hand and led me into the cavernous living room. There was a fire roaring from the richly carved marble fireplace. Its heat warmed me from six meters (twenty feet) away.

There were candles everywhere, large ones on the floor, smaller ones in wrought iron candelabras, small ones on flat stones on the tables. Must have been hundreds of them all releasing the most delightful scent. It reminded me of the Christmas Eve midnight mass of my childhood with white candles everywhere.

The beautiful hand-painted wallpaper was peeling in places. The furniture was from the French Empire period. All had seen better days a hundred years before. The walls had hand carved hardwood accents between the wallpapered sections. The walls were covered with pen and ink portraits of courageous mounted men charging with their armor, javelins, and their fulsome flowing beards. The well-dressed women from the same age as their brave knights were demurely drinking tea in gardens of flowers and peacocks.

The entire salon was a time capsule from a long-lost era. The ceiling was three stories high, capped with a broad horizontal flat window that let in the light of the sky, whether stars, moon, or sun.

There was a long wooden dining table with dishes and bottles arranged in expectation of a memorable dinner.

Besides the normal leather sofas between lacquered side tables, what grabbed my attention was an enormous four-post bed covered in a silky white diaphanous cloth flowing all around it near the far wall where the light did not quite aluminate. That was where I intended to spend the night.

In the opposite corner from the bed, equally dimly lit and barely visible, was a tall statue that appeared to be a nude woman staring down from about three meters (ten feet) above. It somehow fit in with everything else.

She let me take all of this in, knowing that I was thoroughly impressed. As for her, she exchanged her normally white cape and coat for something much bolder. Her sheer silk robe was a riot of colors that formed shapes of something Gustav Klimt would have created if he had smoked a certain noble herb. The candlelight revealed that she was not wearing anything else underneath.

My staring must have reminded her to take the evening slower. She had not let go of my hand since she led me in only five minutes before, but already seemed like hours to me.

"Come over here and sit by the fire. Warm yourself from what must have been an awful wait, you poor dear." She poured out a dark, rich liquor from an ornate antique canter into a museum piece art nouveau crystal glass. There were plates with slices of cheese and of aged smoked black pork (porco preto) from free-ranging pigs that fed on a type of chestnut.

"Come, sit down. Don't be shy. Tell me a wondrous story."

The story of my life was full of sordid tales rather than wondrous stories. I was sure she did not want to hear a sordid tale, so I made up a story so wondrous it was a fairy tale. As the warmth of the fire and the liquor took hold, my story sounded more like the current situation. As I was about to finish with the two lovers alone in an ancient manor by a fire with a large four-post bed, she stopped me.

Art Deco stain glass window

"Hm, I think I know how this adventure will end. Is that how you want this evening to end?"

I looked deep into her eyes and whispered, "Yes. Yes, I do."

"Well, that would be a delightful fairy tale indeed. Come, I have prepared a traditional Portuguese dinner for us." She took my hand and led me to the well laid-out dining table beyond the line of sofas.

"Here, sit next to me. Let me service you. Oh no, I meant serve you. Forgive me. You know English is not my native language."

That was a Freudian slip I would have made. Our hearts were clearly aligned.

She took a large serving spoon sized sample of five dishes and quickly covered my plate. She did the same for herself. Then she poured us two glasses of wine.

"Foreigners are mostly familiar with our Douro wines, but I think you will find this Alentejan one deeply exquisite. Chin chin, as we say here." She slowly clinked her glass with mine. "Here's to the start of our wonderful fairy tale."

I did my usual little ritual when tasting a new wine: hold the glass up to the light to inspect the colors, swirl it around, place my nose almost into the glass to take a deep breath of the complex aromas, take a sip, roll it around my mouth, inhale without swallowing to let the flavors envelop my tongue, then finally allowing it to slip down my throat. All the while I was thinking that success was well within my grasp.

She was definitely taking the lead and not making me do any work at all. I decided to be as putty in her hands and just enjoy the ride. I concluded that I liked this European style of dating and mating.

Deciding to take my mind off plans for later, I concentrated on the food in front of me. Though I was famished, I forced myself to eat slowly and savor the food. And the food! There was grilled octopus, roasted squid, sauteed tiger shrimp, a fillet of a meaty sharklike fish, and clams in white wine and garlic. That was just what was on my plate to start.

After I cleaned my plate, she served from the other five ceramic urns. I pushed back and politely declined.

"No thanks. That was wonderful, but I don't want to eat anymore. I mean, I don't want to overeat." I immediately regretted my last sentence.

"You don't want to overeat? Why? What are you saving space for? Ah, I know. You're afraid that with a very full stomach you will not be able to perform so strongly. Is that it?"

"No, no, that's not it at all!" I blurted out, feeling my face becoming red. I was starting to fear that I still had plenty of time to screw everything up. But she came to the rescue.

"Well, silly boy. Don't you worry about that." She lightly touched my lips with her finger. "I am sure you will perform exceedingly well. Besides, I will be right beside you, accompanying whatever music you decide to play. Having played many instruments, I am very experienced in coaxing the best performances from the lead musician. You men are so silly with your ridiculous anxieties."

Her smile convinced me I truly did hear that right. I smiled in reply and nodded for her to fill my plate again. She replaced it with a clean one and filled it with grilled lamb, huge roasted turkey legs, pork ribs, beef tongue, and suckling pig with crispy skin.

She poured the wine freely, and I was starting to wonder if we might have to save the performance for another night. We talked about many things, mostly about me. She was very taciturn about herself but was deeply interested in everything I had to say, asking questions, and wanting more details all the time. Since everyone likes to talk about themselves, after all it is their favorite subject, I continued along.

Eventually, I decided to stop being an egoist and try to talk about her, including learning her name. All I could gather was that her six grandparents and parents all came from different countries in Europe. She was born here, educated there, grew up somewhere else, married for a time in a different place (thanked the gods she had no children with him), finally ending up back here. I asked her many times what to call her. She replied each time that the less I knew about her, the better. Instead of turning me off, it just made her even more intriguing.

Time sped by quickly. I must have been there for a few hours already. I did not dare look at my watch for fear she would notice and be offended, rightfully so. Fortunately, after several weeks of going to sleep after 0300 to avoid the banshee-like sounds in my place, I was still going strong. A month earlier I would have fallen asleep in my chair.

When she offered dessert, I told her an old port wine would be a great way to finish such an incredible meal. She slid back her chair, took my hand, and led me over to the same set of chairs by the fireplace, saying "What a great idea. I have just the thing."

She wheeled over a wooden cart covered in crystal decanters of every shape and size. She poured into two glasses the most exquisitely rich, deep vermilion liquid and offered me one. I did my typical new wine ritual. It was like nectar of the gods. The rich, complex flavor was such that I thought it a shame to even swallow it and just leave it on my tongue.

"Incredible! What is that?"

"You like it? This is a special port that I keep for special occasions." She paused with a smile that set my heart racing.

She held up my hand, caressed my palm with her lips and continued. "Like this one with my special new friend. It was born in 1958 in the Douro River valley in the north. It has been waiting all these years to make friends with you. Please have more, I have plenty of different ones, all with unique personalities."

Our conversation turned into sweet talk, the kind that lovers indulge in when alone. I was wondering how to proceed. Should I sit back and wait for her to consummate her plans, whatever they were. Or should I start taking the lead as any man should in this situation? I leaned towards being a man and taking control.

I suggested maybe we should take our conversation somewhere more comfortable, like on that very inviting bed over there. She leaned close to me, fondled my ear, and kissed me slowly on my neck. Then she whispered, "What's the rush? Let's relish every moment together. Besides, I think it would be wonderful if we bathed ourselves first. It has been a long day for both of us. Come with me."

She led me to an adjoining room also lit by myriad candles. A marble pool of glimmering water surrounded a high alabaster fountain that was bubbling water down its several steps. Marble sculptures of nubile nymphs surrounded a majestic manly Neptune lounging on top. Then things started becoming truly weird.

CHAPTER TEN

The warmth of the decadently pagan fountain and pool filled the room with steam. For a place with no visible heating besides the fire in the fireplace in the next room, it occurred to me how strangely warm both large rooms were.

I was about to learn just how heated the water was. She kneeled before me and removed my shoes and socks. Then she undressed the rest of me, purring the entire time. I stood by the pool completely nude. With a slight twist of her body, her multi-colored robe slid off her. Before me was the most perfect example of a woman that I could imagine.

"I noticed how much you like my robe. I'll have one for you the next time we meet. And I am sure we will meet again and many times after that."

Her words barely made an impression on me as my mind struggled to take in the goddess who stood before me. She placed her robe on a nearby marble bench and plucked up a silver bowl. It was filled with multi-colored powder. She took my hand with her other and led me into the pool, up to our knees. The water was as warm as a sauna.

She took up some powder in her fingers and intoned a chant from a language I could not even grasp where it was from. She chanted a few lines and then tossed it into the water. At once, the powder produced a colorful mist.

Then she led me deeper into the pool, to where the fountain rose above us with its strange nymphs and other denizens of the sea. There the pool was waist deep. She pulled me down beside her until we were sitting in the water up to our chins.

The powder must have been a special oil-based incense that did not dissolve in water. The water's fragrance filled my nose with a combination of everything wonderful: of flowers and fruit, of spices and perfumes, of musk and sex. Everything altogether was producing the desired effect on me.

"Before I lay with a man, I want him to be clean and fragrant everywhere. And I mean everywhere. If you don't mind, let me wash you."

Being still completely speechless, I could only nod my head in agreement. She scooped up some of the floating incense pools and washed me everywhere, as she promised. Just as I almost lost it, she told me to hold my breath, dunked me under the water, and washed my head.

Holding my breath calmed me down somewhat. I remember thinking during my third dunking that I would not allow any whips, midgets, or handcuffs. The way things were going, it seemed anything was possible.

Things became tough for me again when she told me to wash her. I hesitated, but for only a moment. I softly caressed her, running my hands all over her smooth alabaster skin, using the natural cleansing properties of the magic water. I felt her beauty and was glad to know that she was real, and I was not dreaming. She clearly enjoyed my hands caressing her body. I was beside myself with desire for her right then.

In a sensual teasing voice, she said, "Well, I see that you had no reason to be concerned about over-eating or drinking too much. He seems to be suffering. Let's ease the pressure, shall we?"

She sat me on the lower step of the fountain and straddled my lap. Her fantastic, perfect breasts stared right into my eyes and her beautiful amber red hair streamed down on my face. I will not go into any more details, as they were all the most delicate and intimate kind.

Suffice it to say, she blew my mind. I felt like I was a spaceman driving my rocket straight into the heart of the sun. She had me completely in her power. I was clay in her hands as she crafted the perfect vessel. I would have done anything for her. Whips, midgets, handcuffs would all be welcome.

Our hearts were both racing, hers pounding against mine. She clutched me so tightly that I thought I might be crushed. Slowly, she released her grip and became soft in my arms. Her hard breathing eventually became like a soft whisper in my ear. The reality of time and space gently forced themselves into our conscience.

"You were amazing! God, I would follow you to the ends of the earth, nay, even to the gates of hell itself!" My voice rose to a shout. "You are the most wonderful woman I have ever known. You are perfect. A dream, a fantasy, come true!"

"Yes, it was a beautiful experience. I believe you, but please do not follow me to the gates of hell, even if I were to lead you there."

"If you did, I would gladly go with you."

"Now that we have this wonderful thing established between us, we can think about other things besides the obvious."

"Oh, I agree! We can now think about a relationship, a future together." As soon as I said that my next thought was perhaps I was being too hasty with that comment. After all, I was just finishing a terrible relationship. Merely a few weeks later, I was promising a new woman that I would follow her anywhere, even to hell itself.

I never promised my Ex that, though we did promise to love each other "until death do us part". Indeed, she did not love me in good times, let alone bad. I was shocked that I was even thinking about such things, with this wonderful goddess still astride my lap, holding me tightly inside her.

At last, she relaxed her grip, rose from me, and drew me back into the deeper part of the pool to wash ourselves. Gently, she led me out of the steamy, sparkling waters. She dried me with a thick white towel and invited me to do the same for her with another one.

While we were still nude, she led me back into the main room to the strange statue of the voluptuous nude woman that I saw earlier. The light of a circle of candles flickered dimly from below her outstretched arms.

The well-formed body of the woman would have been perfect in an Art Nouveau version of a classical Greek temple in the garden surrounding the mansion of a wealthy eccentric gentleman from the late 19th century. But her head! It was clearly the head of a fox carved in the style of a Japanese Kabuki mask. The combination was a truly bizarre contrast.

She pulled us down to kneel on cushions she had placed at the goddess's feet. She told me to close my eyes and pray. I asked her how and for what. She replied I should empty my heart and mind. Remove any resistance and let the Fox Spirit enter. I understood her to mean to meditate with an empty mind rather than praying, which filled the mind with supplication or praise, like they do in church.

She began to hum or chant in an incomprehensible language. It seemed to be an Asian language. Was it Japanese? I could not tell, but I found her chanting hum was enveloping my heart, giving me an intense peace. A great light filled my mind.

After maybe fifteen minutes, she reached over and held my hand. Her touch sent a surge of electricity throughout my body that pleasantly buzzed my every fiber. All my senses appeared to be a hundred times more acute. I could hear the waves as if I were on a beach. I could smell each individual candle in the room. I could see every chisel cut on the goddess towering above me. I could feel every one of my strands of hair resting on my skin.

She continued for about another fifteen minutes until she abruptly stopped and released my hand. Immediately my senses returned to their normal quasi numb state. We continued kneeling in silence, and thoughts crept slowly into my mind.

What was I doing? Was she converting me into a strange cult? If it were a cult based on sex, I could accept that. But what did it require in return? Was I supposed to sell my soul? Would I receive eternal youth in exchange? That might be a fair trade, I considered. Or was it a Faustian bargain? I reminded myself that a short time earlier, I promised that I would follow her to the gates of hell.

She broke the silence and abruptly stopped my fecund fertile mind's meandering. "And no, you do not need to sell your soul to be a devotee of my goddess. Well, our goddess now."

Was she really able to read my thoughts? Or was she just answering a question anyone would have asked themselves in the same situation? Was it a mere coincidence? The longer I was with this strange woman, the more mysterious she became.

We rose, and she dressed us in white robes as rich and soft as any I ever wore before. It reminded me of a luxurious bathrobe that reached to the floor.

"It has been a long evening. Come lay with me in bed. Let us sleep with our limbs entwined like the vines covering the walls of the garden." We moved to the large four-post bed covered in a white sheer cloth.

The feeling of the electrical current was still a remnant coursing through my veins. I found my second wind. She noticed and turned me on my back. She mounted me with her long hair falling on my face, framing her magnificent breasts heaving above my eyes.

It was even better than the first time in the pool. With eyes clenched, my mind was being swept up by the incredible physical sensation of joining my body with hers. When I nearly released the incredible pressure building inside me, I opened my eyes. Her face had transformed into that of a fox, a Kabuki fox with dark ebony eyes.

My eyes shut tightly again as I allowed the waves of pleasure to release both body and mind. When I reopened them, she resumed her usual appearance. I certainly had a fertile imagination.

She laid her head on my chest that must have been pounding to her ears as my heart slowly returned to normal. She was humming again, but very melodious and just barely audible. Was she purring? Do foxes purr?

We rolled over on our sides with our limbs indeed entwined, as she said. Normally, I could never sleep so entwined, but sleep was indeed rolling over me like a comforting tropical wavelet. She had pulled a thick heavy blanket over us. It was the fur of a large animal, perhaps a bear skin. Her sweet breath blew so softly on my ear like a mother murmuring a lullaby to her baby. I faded quickly into a deep sleep.

I had the most vivid dream. I was running after her through a verdant rain forest path. She was running so fast that I could never quite catch up to her. Our jungle chase ended when we entered a clearing before a crimson red pool like the one we shared after dinner, except for the color. Colorful birds and monkeys chattered in the trees above us.

Then it struck me that we were not in a tropical Brazilian forest, but rather in a highly stylized tropical garden of an Henri Rousseau painting. Standing beside a towering, imposing tree, nearly hidden in the shadows, a sinister figure played a flute, while a large, dark serpent twisted around him from his head to the ground. The flute created the sounds of the birds and monkeys I heard, invisible in the trees above me.

Behind him was a large wooden gate with wrought iron bands crossing it. A dark, tarnished brass knocker in the shape of a rapping hand dominated the center. Strangely, there were no walls on either side. It was a securely locked gate guarding the entrance to another dimension that required no walls to protect. As for her, she laid nude on a divan in the clearing beside the crimson fountain while strange shadows danced on her breasts.

CHAPTER ELEVEN

The morning's damp cold awoke me. It took several moments to collect my thoughts, trying to remember where I was and how I came to be there. My winter army coat, which I kept after my military service in Korea was finished, covered me like a blanket, yet a chill still pierced me. I realized it was only me in the deserted room. Suddenly I remembered everything and sat up bolt upright. Where was she?

The late morning light seeped through the cracks of the boarded-up windows, providing a dim illumination of the curious room. The candles had all long since burned out. She was nowhere to be seen. She was gone. I was alone.

She had cleaned up everything while I was sleeping. The dining table was bare, and the wonderful booze cart had disappeared. I quickly put my clothes on and fell back onto the bed. The strange fox goddess was just visible in the dim corner. She looked forbidding, even somewhat frightening now.

Getting a grip on myself, I approached her majesty and kneeled at her feet. This time I did pray. I prayed fervently to be reunited with the wonderful unnamed woman who satisfied my every fantasy. She was as perfect as Aphrodite herself.

I still did not know my love's name. So, I prayed for the fox goddess to tell me her name. To give me a sign of her power. I received nothing, just a stony stare from high above me. Standing up with a sigh, I decided I needed to control myself and not lose my mind over her.

Hunger reminded me of more mundane things. I took a quick walk around the room looking for a sign or at least a clue of her whereabouts and, more importantly, when we would meet again. The doors leading off the room were all solidly locked, except for the front door.

I was about to leave when something white caught my eye at the side table of the bed. I approached and picked it up. "you can call me Only After Dark" was written in highly stylized gothic letters. Ah, a name! At last, I had her name, admittedly a strange one, but at least something to hang my mind on. It was probably a nickname. But I did not care, as I would have called her anything she wanted.

Picking up the card, I would have stuck it in my bodice if I had one, right next to my heart, like the ladies did in the old movies. Instead, I placed it carefully in my wallet.

Suddenly the thought struck me that the goddess answered my prayer, after all. That made me stand in silence staring at her in the dark corner, pondering in reverence my new religion. A god never answered any prayer of mine before. It was a small prayer and a small show of bestowal. But it was a start and good enough for me.

My grumbling stomach reminded me it was time to leave. I walked the seven blocks back to my place. I made hot coffee and oatmeal. Sitting in front of a fire in the grand fireplace in the salon, I wrapped myself in a blanket and had my breakfast, warming myself from a shivering chill. Was I coming down with a cold? That was the last thing I wanted, just as things were finally starting with her. Her? I meant with Only After Dark.

The fire and blanket were not enough. So, I made a steaming hot bath. I laid in it with only my nose above water. When the water cooled, I returned to my bed and slept the rest of the day. Clearly, I had overexerted myself the night before. But what a night it was!

As the short day's light was waning, I wondered how we were to meet again. She left no note regarding that. The thought that it was only to be a one-night stand made my heart race in a near panic. Nonetheless, my exhaustion lulled me to sleep.

Five hours later, the moon was rising when I awoke. Luckily, my chill was gone, and I felt better. My next problem in terms of importance was my starving stomach was growling again. I bundled up and went out to find one of my favorite local restaurants for a serious dinner.

After a dinner of a thick seafood stew with rice and a bottle of excellent Alentejan wine, I could rethink my next move. That clearly was to find my Only After Dark. I returned to her home and saw it dark again. The front door was locked, and there was no answer to my knocking. I haltingly returned to my favorite bus stop and waited for an hour. Still, no sign of life manifested itself.

My next thought was to return to our bench by the sea. Perhaps she would 'feel' my presence there and find me. I had no telephone, and she did not know where I lived. It was after midnight. The night's dampness found its way inside my coat and started me shivering.

I felt a chill to my bones and realized that I had to get into my warm bed fast or I would catch a serious cold. All those late nights in the damp chill of a Portuguese winter reminded me that fox goddess or no, I was not immune from the effects of microbes and a weakened constitution.

Despite being chilled, I resolved to return to the bench by the sea, just in case she was there waiting for me. I had to pass my place on the way. As I did so, I had a fit of sneezing over a dozen times. I knew then that my trip to the seaside would have to wait. I was so exhausted that though it was only 0100, I went to bed hours before I normally did and fell into a deep sleep. It was so deep that I did not hear the usual moaning and clanging of chains in the hallway.

The next morning, I felt better and was happy that I had narrowly missed catching a cold. Having a strong constitution, I rarely caught colds anyway. This was also because I was sensitive to the first signs of illness and quickly did something about it. I decided to stay in bed and drink lemon tea with honey for the rest of the day.

As I did so and the hours passed, my memories of Only After Dark continued to push out any possibility of other thoughts. My memories soon turned to the expectation of our next encounter. Expectations turned into yearnings.

It was too much. I dressed warmly and walked through the decrepit palace. I visited the strange old man upstairs. He would be an excellent distraction. Unfortunately, he did not answer my loud knockings. I looked for more cracks that the wind was using to keep me awake at nights. I found more, but I still felt too weak to do any repairs.

I was afraid to go out and eat dinner in a restaurant, as I would be tempted to follow that with hours sitting by the cold ocean. I stayed at home for a few days eating up whatever I had in the pantry, mostly canned food and rice. But even my little stock of canned and dried food soon ended. At the least, I had to go to the market to restock.

The traditional market in Cascais was always bustling with energy and would be the perfect distraction. The sights, smells, and people were excellent entertainment. I soon had two sacks full of fresh food. As I headed for the exit to start the thirty-minute walk home, I saw her! She was on the other side of the market with a hundred people between us.

Just as in the casino a long week before, I could not quite catch up to her. I was shoving people out of my way, causing a scandal. I did not care in the slightest. Ten more seconds! I only needed ten more seconds to catch her. But she disappeared into a waiting Bentley. The chauffeur closed her door and sped off the moment I frantically approached her car window.

She obviously did not see me, or did she? If she did and chose to ignore me, what did that mean? My mind was thrown into turmoil for the rest of the afternoon. Even the walk along the impressive Paredão could do nothing for me. I barely noticed the heaving ocean and its crashing waves slamming into the rocks below.

I muttered to myself the whole way: I must have her! I must possess her! I need her! I concluded we had to live together. We must be together every night and all day, too. I acknowledged that she, in fact, possessed me. It was far beyond physical. She possessed my mind as well as my body.

Yet, I knew next to nothing about her. What did she do during the day? Did she work? She clearly had money to own a mansion in Estoril, no matter how derelict it was. She had a chauffeured Bentley. That counted for something, too.

We had to live together. Should I invite her to live with me? I answered myself that my new home was hardly the kind of place to invite a woman. What about me living with her? The decaying house of our wonderful first adventure certainly required serious repairs. I could do that. My latest book would soon give me enough money to afford to do so.

The thought of my just-published book brought me back somewhat from the edge I was racing towards. I tried to distract myself by considering plots for my next novel. But they all strangely ended up involving her. It was hopeless. I could think of nothing else.

Back in my apartment, a part of me was frightened of the strength of my feelings. I supposed it was my head fighting with my heart. I let that fight continue for the rest of the day until a third player entered the fray. My stomach announced that it was too long since its last proper meal.

While waiting until dinnertime in Portugal (never before eight in the evening), I occupied myself by choosing which restaurant and what I would order. When the time finally came, I dressed well for the weather and found my way to my favorite restaurant in Estoril, an Italian family run place opposite the casino.

Walking the Paredão towards Cascais in the winter.

As I started with my usual entradas and had my first glass of their excellent house wine, I realized that my sly heart had enlisted the aid of its neighbor, my stomach. Before my mind knew it, I had decided to go for a walk on the Paredão afterwards.

The heart nearly always wins in such conflicts. It can recruit the help of its neighbors such as the stomach and especially the organs of sex. The mind really does not have a chance. By the time I had paid my bill and started towards my favorite seaside bench, I realized that the question was answered firmly in favor of Only After Dark.

The ocean was restive, but the night was calm. As I leaned back on the frigid wooden bench, I could see the moon and a few stars peeking out from the overcast sky. I knew she would come to me. I just had to wait. I no longer even cared how long it would be. I would have slept on that bench if needed.

I closed my eyes and remembered our first night. The strange details all crowded into my conscience. My heart was racing at the memory, no longer a fantasy as in earlier stays at my bench. I remembered her every detail, her accent, her breath, the smell of her hair, her perfect body.

The memory of us in the bizarre fountain was arousing me in anticipation. I was completely beside myself in expectation. I did not open my eyes immediately when I felt her presence next to me.

"You called. Here I am, my precious lover."

I could only smile as the heavens opened for me.

CHAPTER TWELVE

Without saying a word, I reached over and hugged her tightly. I began to kiss her passionately, but she pushed my face gently away.

"No, not here, dearest. Let's go somewhere more private."

She led me by the hand along the Paredão.

"I was so worried that I wouldn't see you again. Isn't there some way we can communicate that's better than the random chance we meet at that bench?" I asked.

"I don't know how. There are very few private telephones here. My family owns many homes in this area, and I share my time with all of them. I'm terribly busy, never knowing where I will be or when.

"But don't worry. I'll always make time for you. I promise that I will meet you at your bench at least once a week at this same hour. To make it easier for you, I will always come to you between 2200 and 2300. What time is it now?"

"My watch says 2245." I replied.

"See? It's not too late for you, is it? This way, you don't need to spend all night here worrying about me."

"If that's the best we can do for the moment, I guess that would be fine. But how about if we live together? Then we would have each other all the time and not randomly like now."

"Living together? My, aren't we rushing things! Let's not be so hasty to tear down what we are just now building. Besides, my life is way too complicated these days. I'm working hard to simplify it, but I'll need more time. Let's not talk about such things until then. Please be patient with me. I promise you will not regret it."

"It's another man, isn't it? You have another man. Fine, I can live with that."

"Another man? Don't be ridiculous! I've had many terrible relationships in my past. You have convinced me to try again. I want a simple life with one man and that man is you. No, no, not at all. I just have many family matters to attend to. The Socialist Revolution of a few years ago has made everything for families like mine very complicated."

"How so? Tell me what you are doing. Maybe I can help. I know almost nothing about you, yet you know everything about me. Tell me about yourself. Please!"

"Oh, trust me. The less you know, the better. And I do mean trust me. Do you trust me?"

"I trust you completely! I only want to be a part of you." I nearly shouted.

At once I thought how ridiculous that sounded for someone I just met a few times before. But in my heart, I really did mean it. I told her I would follow her to the gates of hell the last time we were together. I still meant it.

She pulled my hand to her breasts and whispered in my ear, "You are already a part of me. Let's enjoy the sound of the waves and not talk."

The caress of her beautiful breasts calmed my mind of random thoughts and silly words. They were replaced by a single desire for her. The rhythm of the busy waves helped, and we walked in silence. I decided to let her do all the talking. Things would be much simpler that way. The last thing I wanted to do was to say something stupid and drive her away.

We walked for nearly fifteen minutes along the ocean and turned left through a tunnel under the railroad. Another ten-minute walk up the hill on the other side brought us to an old iron gate between two crumbling walls. She unlocked it and led me up the path to the front door. She opened it and motioned me inside. My heart was racing with anticipation.

Past the foyer was another large room like at the previous house, also lit up with many dozens of candles. As before, there was a well-stocked dining table, a fireplace with a fire, a large bed in the corner just like in the first one. My spirit went a bit cold when I could barely make out in the far corner the enormous statue of the strange fox goddess.

There it is again. What exactly have I got myself into? I wondered. At least my strange friend could explain what this religion was all about. She seemed to want me to take part in it, whatever it was.

In my limited studies of world religions, I never encountered anything like this. Was it an ancient fertility cult? But why the head of a fox? I decided to go to the public library in Cascais in the coming days and see what I could learn.

I changed the direction of my thoughts and asked her, "How did you have all of this prepared so quickly for me, or rather for us?"

"There are many who serve me. They leave the important things for me. You will never see them as they are very professional and work from the shadows."

"But what is it that you do? Can I help?"

"No, you can't help me. These are things only I can do. The simple answer to your question is getting my life and the complicated affairs of my clan in order. As soon as I can finish everything, we can spend all our time together. Now join me by the fire for a few drinks and hors d'œuvres."

One of her ruined houses 45 years later.

"Yes, of course. The layout of this place appears the same as the previous one." I started with some small talk.

"Yes, my people liked the interiors of our homes to be identical. The exteriors are different. They reflect the taste of the times a hundred or more years ago. Now try this liqueur. It's a mixture of oranges and honey. I made it myself."

"That is simply heavenly. How do you make it?"

"I start with aguardente, a type of distilled spirit. The aptly translated word in English would be 'fire water'. Then I add the orange skins with the honey. I let it sit for maybe six months and then filter out the solids. I don't know about 'heavenly', but I agree it's not of this world. Here, try this cheese I bought it especially for us. It's made from sheep's milk. To me, cheese from sheep's milk is better than the rather bland cow's milk and the sometimes too sharp goat's milk. Try it on this piece of bread from Mafra."

They say a woman wins a man's heart through his stomach. Was she trying to do that? It would have been a waste of time, as she already had my heart. Women had always won my heart from an organ further below the stomach.

"What can you tell me about this religion you follow?"

"Which religion do I follow?"

"You know. The one with that statue of the fox head goddess in the corner."

"I wouldn't call that a religion. It's not so complicated with all the dogmas and baggage of what I understand 'religion' to be."

"What does she demand from her devotees?"

"She demands nothing. You give her only exactly as much as you want to give and no more. Not one iota more. You will discover over time that you will try to please her in every way you can imagine, completely voluntarily."

"But how do I please her? How do I serve her?"

"You please her by simply pleasing me. Would you like to do that?"

"Do you mean by serving you? Are you her priestess?"

"Serving? That's a strong and loaded word. My servants serve me. That's their job. As for us, we take from each other exactly what we want to give the other. We give to each other exactly what we want to and no more or less. It's quite simple."

"But what is with the fox head?"

"Foxes are extraordinary animals, mysterious spirits of the forest, mystical guides to fantastic worlds. Don't try to analyze it. You'll only end up in a dead end. Come, enough of chattering. Let's take a nice warm bath together. Your body seems tense and nervous. Let's relax it, shall we?" she purred.

She had my full attention as she led me to the familiar fountain in the next room. She dropped her multicolored robe to the floor, revealing her natural beauty, and slowly undressed me. She threw a different colored powder into the warm water, producing a pleasant but different fragrance. Leading me by the hand, we took the same position as our first night together.

I had been dreaming of the very thing for what seemed an eternity. As she lowered herself onto me, I had to control myself to give her the pleasure she so urgently craved. She whispered in my ear, "Now, tell me, my lover, do I have your body?"

"Yes, yes, you do indeed have my body. It's yours whenever you want it, however you want it, and for as long as you want it." Came my trembling reply.

"I want it forever."

"Forever!" Immediately, my capacity for thought completely left me, and I surrendered to the incredible pleasure that she was giving me. I felt like I was in a whirlpool of the most fragrant water that was pulling me gently down into ecstasy. I gave in to its gentle but urgent pull.

Once full conscience returned, she said, "Come, my man. I have a present for you."

She led me out of the pool and dried me off. She reached for a package on a nearby chair. She unwrapped it and clothed me in a most beautiful multicolored robe, just as she promised before. The silky touch tingled my skin. But on closer inspection I discovered that, rather than a fine silk, it was made from thousands of exotic bird feathers.

"As I told you, I would give you a robe like mine. But you can only wear it with me. It has magic and it will make you strong, a strong man. It comes from our goddess. Now we must thank her for the gifts she has given us."

We entered the next room and kneeled before the magnificent statue towering above us. She again chanted her strange incantation. I tried to hum along. She nudged me on my side to silence me. Looking up from below to the large fox face above me, I saw it was smiling. Was it always smiling? A great peace spread through me, and my mind went blank.

After nearly thirty minutes of this, she rose and led me to the dining table, again laden with many wonderful dishes. They were hot, so they must have been placed there while we were praying to the fox spirit. I did not hear a thing. Her servants were truly professional, or perhaps invisible.

"Now you simply must tell me how you like this special wine I found to share with you." She filled our glasses from a crystal decanter.

She raised her glass and tapped mine. "Chin chin, as we say here. To us!"

"To us!" I repeated.

It was wonderful wine, as was the dinner. She encouraged me to eat and drink more than my full. Apparently, her cult was a very sensual and sensuous one. It was a pleasure to all senses, both within and without. I was a devotee, believing in what, I still was not sure. Perhaps it was a cult that required no thinking at all? It would be hard to turn off my mind, but with her I would do anything.

After dinner we laid together, covered in her strange animal skin. We shared each other's bodies again. The details were just as fantastic, if not more so, than the first time. I leaned back, panting, waiting for my heart to stop pounding. My arms held her tightly against my chest. Her heavy breathing filled my ear while her hair spread across my face.

As I fell asleep with her still laying on top of me, I felt her whisper in my ear. "Yes, I do have your body, my precious. What's next?"

I asked her the same question, when I caught up to her in the same Henri Rousseau jungle I dreamed of before. She only turned away from me with her beguiling smile and continued running down the narrow trail. I could only follow her. She stopped in the same forest clearing.

Instead of laying on the divan, she was standing behind an alter by the fountain. She motioned for me to lie on it. I dropped my robe. In the nude, I laid on the strangely warm, white marble altar before her.

The sinister dark flautist, with his face hidden by a monk's hood and wrapped in the same shadowy serpent, stopped playing the wild animal sounds. He changed to a melody that was both forlorn and rhythmic. The same mysterious door with no supporting walls stood behind him.

She poured pungent oil over my body from a large brass vessel. Then she massaged me from my feet to my head. Her touch rejuvenated me like she was charged, transferring her electric energy to me. She was arousing me. I could feel the tension rise as she took me into her mouth. Her electric charge was clearly working on me. As she pleasured me, someone unseen was gradually raising the voltage. Before it became unbearable, I awoke.

CHAPTER THIRTEEN

It was raining when I woke up nude under my Korean War great coat. I could hear the rain falling outside in the winter gloom. The burned-out candles outlining the room were barely visible. In the deepest, darkest corner of the room, I could just make out the towering fox goddess with her outstretched arms. I resolved to find out more that day about the strange cult I had entered.

I dressed myself and sat back on the bed. I surveyed the room for any note or sign from Only After Dark. And, yes, there it was. On the glass protecting a painting on the wall by the fireplace were words formed in the dust. I looked closer and the words: "Remember Only After Dark!" were clearly visible. I inspected the painting as best I could in the gloom through a layer of dust. The old portrait of a woman looked very much like a younger version of my priestess of the fox goddess cult.

Wandering slowly back home by a different cobbled stone street than the first, I did not mind the rain pouring off my coat and rain hat. The storm fit my mood exactly. Cold rain shrouds everything in a mysterious, heavy, watery mist. Afterwards, it both cleanses the sky and refills the earth with life-giving moisture. My muddled mind felt like it was raining inside, but that soon my life would be pure and clean. The sun would appear and remove the darkness that had settled in my heart.

Back home I showered and warmed myself by the fire, eating my breakfast. It was already after noon. The Cascais library would be open by then. So, I walked along the Paredão to Cascais. I stopped and peered out to the open ocean. The waves were particularly strong that day.

Again, the wails of the drowned ancient mariners of thousands of sunken ships were just audible over the groaning wind. What were they trying to tell me? Were they warning me or beckoning me? With fear in my heart, I shut out their shrill siren calls and turned away.

Continuing my lonely walk to the library, I had hoped that one of the seaside cafes would be open, but none were. The quaint library in its Imperial style two-story house sat by itself in its walled garden across the street from the city market. I remembered it was market day and after my library visit, I would restock my pantry there.

Browsing through the library, I could find nothing in English, nor anything else that looked like it could help enlighten me. I found the librarian and her lone assistant repairing a stack of old hardbound books. Knowing almost no Portuguese, I tried French. But she spoke it with such a strong accent that I could not understand a thing. Finally, I tried English, which thankfully she spoke well.

I explained my dilemma. A 'close friend' of mine had fallen hard for a peculiar cult. I wanted to understand what it was about exactly and if my 'friend' was in any danger. She was interested to hear more. So, I described all the details: always at night, a fantastic fountain where the initiates had sex, followed by chanting in an unknown tongue before a statue of a nude goddess with the head of a smiling fox. From what 'my friend' told me, sex seemed to be the central focus.

The last statement really caught her attention. She asked if perhaps I could introduce her to 'my friend'. She might want to

The Cascais Public Library.

experience this strange cult herself. It could help her research. Her voice revealed the lonely yearning of a spinster librarian.

I responded that I would not do that until I knew it was safe. My burning questions were what do they believe and what was it they were seeking at the end of the mystical journey?

She replied it would take some time, maybe a week. She was woefully understaffed. The Communist and Socialist Parties in control of the government did not believe that things like libraries and even higher education were important. She might have to visit the University of Coimbra, one of the oldest universities in the world, where the key to that kind of esoteric subject could be found. If so, she could only do that on a weekend. She told me to return in two weeks. That was the best she could offer.

I wondered where I could find a full Encyclopedia Britannica in English, perhaps somewhere in Lisboa. There was no rush. I was simply curious. I would wait until the librarian did her research. In the meantime, it was time to go food shopping. There were cafes there, too. I felt that I needed an espresso to put everything in perspective.

Laden with fruit and vegetables, bread and cheese, I sat out of the rain in the semi-circle of little restaurants and cafes adjacent to the busy market. I considered the special situation I found myself in with my peculiarly attractive woman. Our relationship was clearly quite unorthodox, odd really. Was she using me in some way? I could not see how.

She appeared to be very wealthy. If she was using me for my body, well, then, in the words of Bill Withers, "If it feels this good being used, then she can use me until she uses me up". With that conclusion, I decided to not think about it until the librarian's report.

Suddenly, I saw her across the bustling market. I ran to her, but again it seemed everyone was scheming to prevent me from reaching her. Only her back was visible, but her hair and coat left no doubt. She was almost at the open back door of a Rolls Royce this

Cascais City Market with cafes visible in the top left.

time that her chauffeur held open. I was going to miss her again. I yelled out "Hey, Only After Dark! Wait! It's me!"

She stopped and turned to me. It was not her! How could that be? I was so sure. The chauffeur walked threateningly towards me. But just then a policeman grabbed me by the arm. Apparently, I had pushed over a few too many people running after the mistaken woman. After it was clear that we could not communicate with each other, he realized I was simply a stupid, rude foreigner. I bowed and apologized to all and sundry, collected my things, and made a quick exit.

It was pouring rain, and I had bought a lot of groceries. So, I took a taxi back. Again, the superstitious taxi driver rushed away with screeching tires when he saw where I got out. I did not even have time to pay him. So, what if the place was a bit decrepit and bricked up? It was not the gaping maw of hell. It was just me and the strange old man who lived there.

I took a hot bath, lit a fire, and sat down in front of it with a glass of port. First, I considered the simpler thing of why the taxi drivers were so afraid of my place. I could not fathom their fear. Yes, the place made many strange sounds at night. But that was easily explained by the wind blowing through cracks in the window frames. There was always a wind at night.

It seemed that they thought the place was haunted. But I never saw any ghosts or demons. I decided if the strange reputation kept out the derelict drug users, that was fine with me. Besides, they had many other options in the area to use for their self-destructive habit.

But then I came to the much more troubling thought: What the hell was coming over me? Why did I lose control so completely when I imagined seeing her at the market? I was seeing her everywhere: the back of a woman at a restaurant, glimpsing another from the corner of my eye as she passed me on the Paredão, someone else disappearing behind a closing door, etc. I was ashamed of the embarrassing scene I made earlier that day.

Staring into the fire, my alarm slowly merged into a desire to see her again. I decided that I was simply being a fool in love and nothing more. Nonetheless, I had to control myself better. Despite everything, I was very curious about the fox spirit religion. I considered waiting until I received the librarian's report before revisiting my Only After Dark, but I quickly banished the thought.

After a wonderful dinner of baked duck and rice at my favorite casino restaurant, I decided to unwind at the little bar on the second floor. It was the only bar that had windows. From there, one could see the lamps that outlined the front garden that rolled down to the train station and the wine dark, heaving sea beyond it.

My odd, newfound friend was well ensconced at the bar. When he saw me, he motioned me over to the stool next to his. It was precisely what I needed, a friendly someone with perspective. I sidled up and ordered a single malt. It was that kind of day.

"Ah! My friend! I haven't seen you in a while. How are you settling into your new home?" he asked.

I replied that I was settling in nicely and described my relationship with the new love of my life. Without going into too much detail, I briefly described how we met on the Paredão less than two weeks before. I explained how we immediately hit it off and our encounters at her different homes in Estoril.

"Well, that's really excellent news. Tell me. What's her name? I wonder if I know her."

I was happy to know at least that much about her. "Only After Dark. I know it's a strange name, but it probably is an English translation of her name from the original or perhaps just a nickname."

Then I proceeded to tell him what little I knew of her very mixed background.

"I have been living in Estoril off and on for nearly fifty years and I have never heard of such a person, especially if the family owned several homes here. No matter, I can't know everyone. Tell me about your encounters and in which house did you meet?"

I could not tell him addresses and, being instinctively protective, I only gave him vague directions. I described our encounters. Due to my overriding curiosity of the fox spirit cult, I emphasized that part. I concluded with a question, "Have you ever heard of such a cult? That's what I'm most curious about."

He leaned back with a thoughtful expression and lit his cigar. "Let me review what we know. First, a feast, then a ritualistic tryst at the base of a strange fountain, followed by chanting before a tall statue with the nude body of an Art Nouveau woman with the head of a smiling fox. This has happened twice, both times at different houses, and each morning you awoke alone. Hmm, interesting, interesting, indeed.

"Clearly, it's a religion based on physical pleasure. Eating, drinking, a warm bath with a particular focus on sex. Clearly not of Jewish, Christian, or Muslim origin. That makes me consider a fertility cult, something from ancient Greece. But now we must consider the statue of the goddess herself. She was carved in the manner of Art Nouveau. That causes me to guess that it was a pagan cult created by an eccentric rich man in the late 1800's.

"But why the head of a fox? What does a fox represent in Western culture? Cunning, foxes are cunning. They can think of ingenious ways to outfox the farmer and get his chickens, right? Outfox. Of course, if we could understand what she was chanting, that would clear it up. But you say you don't recognize the language. It might not even be European.

"I wonder what is it she's praying for? If it's a fertility cult, she would pray to be fertile and become pregnant, pregnant by you. She could be chanting to give you great power to please her and give her a child. She could be thanking her goddess for the pleasures of life. Does any of that make sense?"

I considered the alarming prospect of making her pregnant. Is that what she wanted from me, after all? I mulled that over in silence for a few moments, but then decided that would be fine with me. I would do whatever, indeed, be whatever my beloved wanted.

I answered, "Not so sure about the pregnancy part. I am in my mid-forties and as beautiful as she is, as perfect as she is, she might even be older than me. I doubt she would want to start a family so late. She was married before and that would have been the time to have children.

"But the idea of a pleasure cult makes more sense to me. You know, something like an Asian Yin and Yang thing, the equal union of opposites. It's all about the union. The pleasure…"

He interrupted me. "Ah, I remember a few years ago. There was a travelling exhibition of Buddhist tantric mandalas from Tibet. Many of them portrayed Buddha as an ugly, fearsome monster with a young buxom beauty mounting him in the sex act as he stood glaring back at us over her shoulder. You might be onto something."

"Yes, I have seen them at the New York Met, too. Even if we reverse the sex of the adherents, that would explain the fox head, though it's definitely not a fierce monster. It has a rather charming, smiling face. And for sure the body is no monstrous man's body. That much I am sure of. Thanks for your analysis, but I think this is something different."

"Unless she thinks you are the monstrous Buddha that she is seeking union with. Besides pleasure, is there anything else she might be trying to get from you? You say she is from old money, a lot of it. You don't think it's to have a baby with you. What else could it be?"

"I really don't know. Maybe my dreams might help." I continued by relating the two strange dreams I had after our time together.

He became quite alarmed after listening to my account. "You told me earlier that you would do anything for her, even follow her to the gates of hell. In both your dreams, there is a weird mysterious character in the shadows playing his magical flute with a serpent wrapped around him.

"The dreams end in a jungle clearing: first with her nude on a divan. The second ended with you on a strange altar and her performing a bizarre ritual on you. You promised her your body when she asked for it. We might be getting somewhere after all. Dreams often reflect the subconscious, which knows more than our conscious does. Could she be a demon entrapping you with pleasure?"

"That's ridiculous. Do you think it's a devil-worshipping cult? The Devil is a gentleman with horns and a tail. Besides, unlike what the Church traditionally believes, we are only two consenting adults enjoying the fruit of our physical senses and that is no mortal sin in my mind. We are doing nothing evil."

"Yet. And by the way, the demons tossed out of heaven were angels and angels are sexless, despite what folklore betrays."

"Well, now you are not being helpful. The truth is she already has my body, and I would gladly give her my heart and mind, too. If she asked for my soul, I would seriously consider that possibility."

"Seems to me you have already decided to go down the slippery path you have chosen."

"Yeah, I guess I have. I was mainly curious about the religion and not asking for advice what to do about it. Let's change the subject." I ordered another scotch.

CHAPTER FOURTEEN

The next morning, I awoke still in my clothes, though I did take off my shoes before falling into bed. I recited to myself the old adage from high school: whisky before beer, never fear. Beer before whisky is mighty risky. I decided it applied to wine as well.

It seemed to me that I was drinking more than usual and regularly. I pondered why I would be doing that now and not during my divorce. I guessed I had enough sense not to drink when I was under great stress. That can never be a good idea. I concluded it was to help me sleep through the night, among the bizarre sounds that filled the corridors. That was the easy answer. I pondered no further.

The shaky start to my morning made me realize I was in no state to entertain or be entertained that day. I puttered around the apartment and the salons. I did not have the energy to even climb the stairs to see if my elderly neighbor was about.

While staring into the fire in the fireplace during lunch, I analyzed why I could write nothing of consequence. This was the time I should be writing my follow-up novel to my just published bestseller. A shop in the casino sold foreign newspapers and I could track my novel's progress in the New York Times.

Of course, the answer was her. I was clearly infatuated with her. I had to admit she played me well. Her intuition had me figured out the first time we met. That she had me wrapped around her little finger was an understatement.

Our relationship, if I could call it that, was strange, I admitted to myself. Everything was great with me so far, even our meetings in her derelict houses, though I must say they were less derelict than the one I called home. But one thing stood out a little uncomfortably. The wonderful but strange rituals with her somewhat unsettling cult.

More importantly, it appeared as if we were on a strange path, an odd journey. But where was it leading? To marriage and a family? That seemed unlikely, though I would have gladly done so, if that was what she wanted. That thought led to the question of what was it she wanted, really?

I changed the subject when I remembered a sizeable amount of money from my advance arrived in my Portuguese bank account. I could move out of the discomfort of my decrepit palace and move into the luxury of the Palacio Hotel next to the casino. I would be leaving one historic palace to a commercial one, though the latter was much closer to a real one than where I was living. It would be a place where I could bring her back. We would not have any fox goddess statues grinning down at us, but we would have a large bathtub to replace her fountains.

Another possibility would be to return to the US and buy a sunny bungalow on a San Diego beach for us. It would be wonderful to make love under the California sunset with the Pacific breezes cooling our heated bodies. I thought that was the better choice.

But what would she want? That question raised its head again. I was becoming impatient. It was time we discussed our future the next time we met. When would that be? I was never certain when she would appear by my side. I would try the following night.

Whatever the case, I would not return to that casino bar. My acquaintance there always had some strange insight which just did not mix well with the facts. How could he know better than me what I was experiencing with that wonderful woman, a goddess herself? Besides, the whisky was way overpriced. Why would I not drink the wonderful Portuguese wine much more reasonably priced at my favorite local restaurant?

The rainy afternoon passed with these and many other random thoughts and questions. The dancing flames had a hypnotic effect on me. Basking in the fire's warmth, I dozed off. I awoke to a door's loud slam down the corridor. My curiosity roused me from my slumber. I went to investigate.

I thought all the doors were solidly locked or even boarded up. This one apparently was not. The wind blew a door open at the end. It was swinging gently to the breeze blowing through a crack in the window.

The late afternoon gloom hid the details of the room's contents. It was an apartment like my own in size and style of furniture. I entered to take a closer look.

To my dismay, I saw in a dark corner a life-sized statue of a hooded woman in a robe holding out a stone lantern. Instead of a smiling fox face, it was a grinning skull face. It was a statue normally found in cemeteries. I wondered who in the hell would want a statue like that in their living room? I admitted to myself it was creepy, but somehow normal for the place.

I closed the door securely and returned to my apartment. I laid off the wine that night and had a light dinner. I read until my eyes grew heavy. Stuffing cotton balls in my ears, I fell asleep early.

Ten hours later, a few rays of the late morning sun, peeking through the dreary rain clouds, shone upon my face and woke me. Looking at my clock, I realized how exhausting my life was, both mentally and physically. The physical part made me smile. I would seek her at the Paredão that night.

Going about my morning, I hummed some tune from 1969. I realized that I lacked music. Music would definitely lighten up my place. A record player needed records. Buying music records that were not Fado would be a daunting challenge in Portugal. The obvious answer was a radio. Surely there would be a music station from Lisboa that would be acceptable.

It drizzled as I walked along the Paredão to Cascais. I withdrew some of my advance money from my bank and found my way to a high-end electronics store. The young store attendant greeted me and asked me what I wanted.

"I am looking for a radio."

"What kind? A small transistor radio with earplugs?"

I thought of my grandfather listening to the Phillies baseball games on his transistor radio. "No, I want something powerful. Something that can both receive stations from far away, but also be loud enough to drive them out of my house."

"To drive whom out, sir?"

"Them. The ones who make all that noise every night." I realized that would make no sense to anyone.

"You mean animals in your attic?"

"Ah, yes, animals in my attic. Do you have anything like that?"

He showed me many large, nearly antique radios that would have been normal in old photos of American families huddled together listening to Roosevelt's fireside chats. I clearly was not in a New York City electronics store, busting at the seams with every modern electronic gadget.

"No, I'm looking for something more modern, like a boom box. Do you know what I mean?"

"Ah, yes, a boom box. These just came in from Japan. Normally, in Portugal, gentlemen of your age prefer more traditional radios for their homes, something akin to a piece of furniture. These are what we young people listen to, but most of us don't have the money to buy them."

"Gentlemen of my age? How old do you think I am? I'll give you a hint. I'm only about twice your age. Oh, never mind. Let me take a look." There were only four choices. I had no cassette tapes, so I did not need the three that had two cassette players. The only other choice suited my purposes.

"Turn the radio on and show me what stations would play rock music. Do you listen to rock music?"

"Of course, sir, that is the only thing my friends and I listen to. We Portuguese are just now discovering rock and roll after decades of Salazar. We still don't have many choices, but this one is the only station that plays just rock. Not like the others that may play it for a few hours a day, between classical and Fado."

"I'll take it."

"Make sure you buy a lot of batteries for when you want to play it in the park. If you get any angry stares from those nearby, do like I do. Close your eyes and just smile, grooving to the music."

"I doubt I'll be playing it in any park. But I'll pick up some batteries, anyway. It's raining. Can you call a taxi for me?" I could have unpacked it, loaded the batteries, and walked back along the Paredão with my boom box on my shoulder booming my message to the world.

"I can't call a taxi, if you mean by phone. But I'll go get one for you." He ran out the door, clearly thrilled to have made such an impressive sale. The price was twice what it would have cost in the US, but I did not mind. I had to wake up my slumbering palace one way or another.

As usual, the taxi screeched off before I could barely shut the back door. This always baffled me, as whatever they were afraid of would not come out to the street and bother a taxi driver. It was raining, so I hurried inside with my new purchase. I set it up in my living room and turned on the station that the helpful young man set it to.

Sure enough, it was exactly what I wanted. The station was playing Santana's entire Abraxas album, one of my favorites of all time and of all bands, his best. The first song that played was Black Magic Woman. I turned it way up so that everyone and everything could hear it throughout the building.

It was late afternoon. I thought at least the music would bring my old neighbor out of his locked lodging to complain about it. He seemed more like a Bach man to me. But no such luck. I let the radio play for four hours, rocking the old palace with the great classic rock from years before. There was none of the new-fangled new wave music like the Talking Heads that nonetheless still strangely appealed to me. The disc jockey knew my music tastes well: simple music with simple lyrics that could rock the soul.

Before I turned it off, there was a loud banging on my door, followed by a roar like the wind would make in a tempest. At last, a reaction from my neighbor! I opened the door and there was no one there. Ah, so he wants to play games, does he? I closed the door and about five minutes later, he did it again. I opened the door and again, no one was there.

He must have been thinking to annoy me since I annoyed him. Old people can be so infantile. After the third time, I entered the corridor and yelled into the empty darkness: "Now you are being silly. Come in for some Port. Let's chat awhile."

There was no answer. I left my door open after that. Would he still knock on an open door? Jefferson Airplane's White Rabbit echoed through the halls. It was already 2100, and the shrieks had not started yet. Maybe at least the shriekers liked the music. I was enjoying the whole experience.

My groaning stomach told me it was time to consider going out for my dinner. So, I turned off the music and left my strangely quiet palace for my favorite local restaurant. I limited my wine intake and afterwards went to the Paredão for my usual study of the Atlantic's rough behavior on a frigid winter night.

I decided that I would be strong and not think about my strange woman. I even sat at a different bench than normal, staring out at the blustery darkness. The approaching waves appeared as a line of Valkyries charging toward a recent battlefield looking for their harvest of dead warrior souls. The white capped sea foam flew backwards from this undulating galloping line, as if the wind were blowing their white hair behind them. Their faces were too blurred, but I imagined they would be the faces of foxes.

This thought amused me for a while until the excesses of the night before reminded me that I should go to sleep earlier that night. I returned to my strange home. The shrieking and other annoying noises had already started. I turned my radio on to drown them out. But I knew I could not sleep to rock. I found a station that was playing Eric Satie and Claude Debussy. I could sleep to that. Though it was not Bach, it calmed them down enough for me to sleep in peace.

CHAPTER FIFTEEN

It was the first time that I awoke before the sun rose since I arrived. Because of that, the day was six hours longer for me than usual. I felt energized from the first good night's sleep I had in weeks. I decided I need to hire a handyman to find the source of all the nightly noise. Was it trouble with the plumbing, a problem with roof insulation letting in the howling wind, or was it something else?

I asked at the Deck Bar for names and phone numbers of such specialists. They gave me about a half dozen. I called them and they were all willing until I told them where my home was. They refused to continue the conversation. Despite my offer to pay twice as much as normal, they still would not accept. They had the kind of fear money could not resolve.

Since plumbing was beyond the scope of my ability, the only thing I could do was try to patch up the cracks and holes that would let in a windy whistle. Unfortunately, I could only enter a few of the rooms. Some doors were unlocked and for others I could open with one of my many keys. I could not open the others because I did not have the key or, if I did, the rusty lock would break. For those, I would have to work from the outside.

The work helped me try to find a balanced mind, but a few days later my spirit started to become restless. A great yearning grew in my heart that spread to my physical being. Those two overpowered my mind and I found my way to my bench by the sea after a late dinner.

Closing my eyes to concentrate on my love, I sensed her presence after about fifteen minutes. Before I opened them, I considered how disappointed she must be in me for not coming for several days. Yet, she came anyway. I opened my eyes and hugged her tightly.

She took me to yet another mansion that was quite different from the others on the outside, but inside was nearly the same. A few details were different, for example, the paintings on the wall and the frontispiece of the fireplace. But the covered four-post bed, the well-laid out dining table, and the goddess – always the goddess.

We went through every action like a well-known and beloved ritual. The sensual dinner, the erotic warm fountain, the fervent time before the fox goddess, followed by another fine romp before falling asleep limbs entwined in her four-poster bed.

There was one change at our feast. Since I recently rediscovered the joy of music, I asked her if I could bring my boombox next time. She looked at me with a distaste that made my heart shudder.

"Did you say, 'boombox'? Please! We are not in the crass USA. Do you mean to listen to your banal disco music while we eat such a classy dinner like your empty-headed teenagers? This is why my friends all question my decision to have an American boyfriend." She looked away with her full rouged lips quivering.

This outburst caused great panic in my mind. I pleaded, "No! No, my dearest! No! I was thinking it would be nice to listen to Beethoven or one of the French Romantics as quiet music in the background. Please forget I said such a silly idea."

"If that's the kind of music you were thinking, I agree it would be a fine addition to our time together." Her voice, once again calm, pacified my racing heartbeat.

She called out in a loud but melodious voice, "Musica, faz favor."

One of her ruined houses 45 years later.

Immediately, someone started playing Beethoven's Moonlight Sonata on a piano in the fountain room. The classical pianist played through dinner and our union in the fountain. We reached orgasm to Rimsky-Korsakov's The Flight of the Bumblebee. A perfect choice by the pianist. But I could not see where the piano was in the gloom of the recesses of the large steamy room.

She clung to me with my head buried in her wonderful breasts and her long amber red hair flowing all around me. I could feel her heartbeat slowly returning to normal. She whispered in my ear, "Do I have your mind now?"

Considering the circumstances, my mind readily agreed that she indeed had it. I whispered my assent while nibbling her earlobe. I knew from that point on, there would be no debate between my mind and the rest of me. I would meet with her every night if possible, banishing any doubts my mind might still be clinging to.

The piano stopped as we knelt before the goddess. I prayed with a new fervent intensity. I was not sure what I should have been praying for. So, I held the goddess's image in my mind, then I concentrated on my Only After Dark's image, praying that the heaven I found myself in would never end, until the two images merged into one.

As we made love afterwards with my eyes tightly closed enjoying the pleasure, I imagined that I was making love to the goddess herself with her sensual smiling fox face breathing heavily on mine, growling softly with ecstasy.

She always exhausted me utterly, leaving me with a soft warmth that quickly pulled me into slumber. My dream was the same as before, except when I was lying on the altar, she was standing nude at the end by my head. Her quim rubbing against my hair smelled of musk from our recent sex. She placed her hands lightly on my head. I felt an electric charge flow through my entire body, making me both numb and fully relaxed. It was incredible! Then I passed out.

As I passed out in my dream, I awoke back into the cold strange world of reality, alone again. It was already mid-morning, and the sun was shining for a change. I rose, dressed myself, and exited the old decrepit mansion.

The dark, nearly empty house was in a part of town I had never been. It took me awhile to find my bearings. Luckily, Estoril is on a hill and going downwards meant eventually I would arrive at the sea. From there, I could find my way back home.

Despite the sumptuous dinner of the previous night, I was already hungry. I stopped at one of my favorite cafes to have a double espresso with a drop of milk and an egg tart with cinnamon.

As I sipped my coffee, I pondered my latest adventure. Everything was perfect, except the strange dreams afterwards. There was something at once sinister, yet pleasurable about them. Could there be such a thing as a sinister pleasure?

Why were the dreams all the same except for the ending? She clearly was the dominant one in the relationship. I was still not sure if I should even use the word 'relationship' yet. I followed her in every detail. She was leading me on a strange journey. But to where and to what end?

She asked me the night before if she had my mind. What a strange question. Of course, she did. There was no denying that it was exceedingly difficult to think of anything but her all day. It was hard to make simple decisions. Ordering from a menu was simply impossible. Certainly, I could not write a meaningful sentence.

For the rest of the day, I felt like I was still in a dream. My reactions to other people, such as a waiter, were in slow motion. I spoke slowly. I walked haltingly, not noticing even if cars were approaching when I crossed a street. I shuffled through the day like a sleepwalker wandering in the night, my feet guided more by habit rather than thought.

After I managed to find my way back home, I decided in a moment of clarity that after a hot shower, I really needed to have a nice long nap. I instantly fell into a deep sleep, dreaming of following her in the same tropical Rousseau forest with the sound of the flute becoming increasingly shrill.

There was no fountain clearing with a divan or an altar at the end. Instead, it was just a long frantic chase through the damp darkness below the forest canopy with threatening, clamoring, chattering monkeys invisible above.

She was always ahead of me, just out of reach. My heart pounded with panic that she might escape me. The path twisted and turned. Because the old-growth trees prevented much sunlight from reaching the ground, there were no bushes and other shrubs blocking my way. She was simply always just a bit faster than me. Her beautiful nude body enticed me to redouble my efforts, but they were always in vain.

My pursuit seemed endless until I woke up when I fell on the floor of my living room in the twilight's gloom. I was utterly naked except for my socks and shoes. My front door was open. It slowly dawned on me that I had been running after her up and down the corridors of the palace for hours in my sleep!

I was thoroughly exhausted and shivering in the coldness of the late afternoon. I was certainly in no state to do anything else but crawl back into bed, pull the heavy blanket over my head, and fall into a deep, dreamless sleep. Everything was clearly taking a toll on my entire being. I slept for fifteen hours until the middle of the next morning, when I awoke with the sun's rays of the new day on my face.

I felt much better physically, but my first thought immediately threw my mind into turmoil. I slept through the night. I missed her! What would she think if she came for me, but I was not there? I wanted to call her and apologize profusely. But since neither of us had a phone, I had no idea how to contact her.

Pacing around my apartment for a few hours anxious how to remedy my near-criminal act, I completely forgot that I had eaten nothing but an egg tart for the entire previous twenty-four hours. An intense hunger brought me back to earth. I calmed down and ate some old bread and cheese with my coffee in front of the grand fireplace, soaking in the fire's warmth.

Fear gripped me in its cold tight clammy hands. My mind raced to find a solution. Finally, the dancing flames gently directed me to a way forward. I meditated the way I did on the cold, wet bench by the Atlantic and conveyed my message to her that I was sorry to have missed her. My heart stopped racing and a calmness spread through me. My meditation turned into prayer. I fervently beseeched the fox goddess herself for forgiveness.

I broke into a low sing-song chant of the sounds that I learned from Only After Dark bowing before our deity, though they were completely meaningless to me. I intoned the syllables to the best of my ability. After an hour or more of this my mind shot alert when I distinctly heard the words: *Musuko yo, anshin sulu. Yurusu koto wa nani mo janai* from someone standing behind me. The words made no sense, but the tone of voice was full of gentle love that a mother would use to calm her crying baby.

My eyes opened, and all was right with the world. My heart floated on this cloud of radiant joy the rest of the day. The joy slowly turned to impatient expectation as the sun disappeared and the night's darkness descended. With a restless mind, I had an early supper at one of the casino restaurants that are open all day, every day.

Afterwards, I paced impatiently around the casino looking for distraction, watching the idle rich steadily lose their money in a variety of entertaining ways. I avoided wine and bars as I wanted to be sober for my meeting with Only After Dark. The witching hour approached, as my mother would call it, and I walked purposely to my rendezvous by the sea.

CHAPTER SIXTEEN

As soon as I sat down on my favorite bench by the sea, I clenched my eyes shut and willed her to come to me. She usually arrived after about ten minutes, but not this time. She had not arrived even an hour later. I was becoming frantic. My panicked heart was pounding. Sweat was pouring down my face. I started to tremble, nearly falling onto the ground.

My head was pounding. I felt like I was in a dark tunnel and a freight train was fast approaching, with its powerful lamp shining on me like a spotlight on a stage. I stood bravely on the tracks, facing my tormentor, waiting resignedly for my doom. As the overbearing light with its angry shrieking whistle was almost upon me, I felt a hand squeeze my shoulder.

Without opening my eyes, I lunged to hug her tightly to me in my desperation. It was a policeman who promptly knocked me to the ground. I was so embarrassed! He was barking at me in Portuguese with handcuffs in his hands. I was so befuddled and ashamed of myself I could hardly respond. I resigned myself to being arrested and held out my hands to be cuffed.

Just then, a woman's voice interrupted us. It was her! She finally appeared. She said something to the policeman, who reluctantly put away the handcuffs. He was clearly angry at my sudden bear hug and was yelling at me, shaking his finger in my face. I was torn between being contrite for my mistake and the ecstasy that she came to my rescue.

She calmed him down with her soothing, silky voice. He walked away. I grabbed her in a tight hug, which she accepted for about ten seconds, until she brushed off my arms.

"What is the matter with you? Why did you attack that policeman? If I had not arrived when I did, you would be spending at least tonight or more in jail instead of with me."

I started to explain but realized I could not. Of course, I did not attack him but mistakenly hugged him, thinking he was her. But that would only make things worse. So, I told her he grabbed my shoulder from behind and I thought he was a mugger.

She replied with a laugh, "Why did I choose a silly American to be my man? You really need to get a hold of yourself. You are not in the US where, as I understand it, such things happen all the time. You must learn to relax. Now come with me. My driver's waiting."

The elation of seeing her emptied my mind of everything else. I barely registered that she mentioned her driver. This was a first. Were we going somewhere far?

We walked through the tunnel to the Marginal, the coastal road that ran from Lisboa to Guincho Beach far past Cascais. There, parked by the side of the road, was her Bentley. The driver had the back door open for us. She climbed in first, revealing that under her ankle-length winter coat she was wearing nothing else. The sight of her bare thighs filled my heart with desire. Now I had that to contend with in my confused mental state.

I pulled her close as the driver slowly drove off. I kissed her bare neck passionately as my hand reached between her thighs. Rather than opening them, she pushed me away with a giggle. "Not now, silly!"

The rest of the trip she spent snuggled in my arms. I calmed down enough to look out the window and try to follow our route, considering I would most likely have to find my way back home alone the next morning. The car stopped under the carriage shelter in front of the entrance to a large dark mansion with its windows bricked up. Even in the gloom of the night, this one appeared in worse shape than the others.

Looking past the horseshoe shaped driveway with tall weeds nearly covering it, I could just see the ocean far down the hill. The moon had broken through the winter clouds, revealing the waves crashing against the rocks below, tossing up wet white curtains of sea foam. At least I knew how to go down a hill. Confidant that I could find my way back home, I turned to her.

She smiled. "Do you like the view?"

"The view of the ocean or of you, radiant in the moonlight?"

"You choose which view to answer."

"I love the view of you, who are both my sun and my moon, my guiding star in the vast, mad emptiness of the turbulent world."

"Is that how you write in your books?" She took my arm, leaned her head against my shoulder, and led me inside.

Past the foyer, I again entered a room similar to the others: hundreds of lit candles, a great spread on the dinner table, a well-stocked liquor cart, the wonderfully inviting four-post bed on the other side of the room, the barely visible goddess standing in her dim corner. It was all there.

My attention was riveted when she hung her coat by the door and the beauty of her nude body filled the foyer like a newly lit light fills a dark room. She put on her colorful robe of feathers. She undressed me and slipped my own colorful feather robe on me. As she pulled the robe down past my waist, she whispered, "Hold on, my stallion. Not quite yet."

With some frustration, I flopped onto the sofa by the warm fire. Handing me a glass of Spanish sherry, she sat beside me. Again, we were alone together. With the weight of her head resting on my chest and a few gulps of the sherry caused a loud sigh to escape my lips.

One of her ruined houses 45 years later.

A great weight of anxiety was removed from my heart like setting down a heavy load after a long walk.

She offered me a plate of goat cheese and a bowl of perfectly cured olives. "So, tell me. How are you? You realize I came for you last night, but you never came. I was worried about you. I never expected to miss you like that. I have never yearned for a man before as I do for you." She caressed my face.

"Oh, my dearest! How I missed you, too. I don't know what came over me. I have been having the strangest dreams about you lately, about us, actually. I was exhausted. I wanted to take a quick nap, but instead I slept fifteen hours right through until this morning."

"Really? Am I wearing you out? Maybe we should cut back on our time together."

"Oh, no, no, my precious! We should spend more time together; I mean all the time together. I think of you. I desire you every minute of the day. It is being apart that is wearing me out."

"Oh, really? Together all the time?"

"Seriously, every minute of the day. I can't think of anything else. The truth is I am obsessed with you."

"I guess I should be flattered that I have a man who is so obsessed with me. Well, just relax. You have me."

Emboldened, I started to talk about practical matters. "Look, I know you're busy every day with your many houses and other matters. Why don't you sell a few of them and simplify your life?"

"Oh, dear man, how I would love that. But the property laws are extremely complicated in Portugal, especially with large families and mine is larger than most. It takes years to get agreement from all the siblings and other family members just to decide a price.

"The government is starting to allow squatters to live in these empty houses. They already started doing that in Lisboa. What do you think I have been struggling to do for the years since the Revolution?"

"Maybe I can help you?"

"Help me? No, you would only complicate everything. If my family knew I had a rich and famous American author as my man, I could get nothing done."

"Then maybe we can at least live together in one of them. Choose one and I will gladly work to renovate it. I would do it with love in my heart. How about this one? I could use my own money to do it."

"Living in any of these old and way too big houses is not my idea of living. My tastes are much more modern than this old stuffy Estoril with its tired casino. No, my idea is to live on a large yacht and sail the world. Do you know how to sail?"

"Oh, I love that idea. I can sail dinghies on a lake. The principles are the same. How much different can it be on the ocean?"

She laughed at that. "Let's discuss this later. I'm famished. Let's have dinner."

Dinner was the usual excellent sensual experience. There clearly was a team of Michelin-starred chefs in a hidden kitchen that produced a meal that fulfilled every desire of the senses with the rich aroma, the visual presentation of the dishes, the texture and the flavors playing joyfully on the tongue. The soothing crackling of the fire completed all five senses.

I was chattering through dinner, partly in relief of being together and partly in anticipation of what was coming next. She gave short replies to my questions and asked me all manner of things in return. Dinner concluded with a second glass of fifty-one-year-old port wine. The intensity of that wonderful experience quieted my restless mind.

My mind became razor focused when she rose and held my hand, leading me into the wonderful next room with its warm bubbling marble fountain. She dropped her robe to the floor, and I did the same, not waiting for her to disrobe me.

Her powder was dark purple this time and smelled of French lilacs. I picked our usual spot in the warm water, leaning my back against the fountain wall for support. In our preferred position, she straddled my lap with her full soft breasts cradling my face and her long fragrant hair covering my head like a wizard's hood. We easily united our hungry bodies, and our heated motion bounded together in a rhythm of urgent waves of passion.

She understood me perfectly. Her rocking would take me close to the precipice, but then she knew exactly how to pull me back in time. She kept at it until I could take it no more. I firmly grabbed her by her hips and took control, bringing us both to climax.

Considering how tightly she clutched my face to her heaving breasts, I was assured I did the right thing. She made a low muffled sound of satisfaction. Was it a groan, a purr, a growl? Slowly our hearts calmed, and our breath returned to normal. While we were still united as one body and she gripped me tightly inside her, she whispered, "Tell me! Do I have your heart?"

I replied hoarsely that indeed she did. She responded by kissing my forehead. Slowly she released me, rose, and led me out to dry me. I dried her, amazed that after so many women and so many years I still could be utterly fascinated by a woman's body. We dressed in our robes and took the customary position, kneeling before the happy lupine goddess.

She started her chanting. But instead of concentrating on the solemn ritual, I was embarrassed by my thoughts wandering to our next romp in bed. I tried hard to concentrate, instead, on the worship of my mysterious new religion.

A vision filled my consciousness of the deity herself approaching me as I laid in bed and made love to me as an ancient goddess would to one of her devotees beseeching her favors in her ancient temple. With a vision like that, I did not have to fight my natural inclinations.

Those natural inclinations were more than satisfied later with my personal love goddess. Strangely, the vision I had with the fox goddess filled my head again as we reenacted my fantasy, kneeling before the grinning goddess. It was no longer a fantasy. I released myself into my goddess and let go of any self-control, falling into the holy sea of pleasure. Her alluring furry fox face smiling down on me with love and passion in her eyes.

This vision blended into a dream. Again, I was chasing her through a jungle trail with Rousseau's flautist playing a shrill dirge in the darkness. The dark locked wooden door without walls framed him from behind. Her swaying hips remained just out of reach. How I wanted to grab them and pull her to me. Lust and desire were propelling me forward.

We reached the same clearing with the same old pagan alter in the center. She turned and motioned for me to climb on top and stretch out upon it. She stood by my head. I breathed in deeply the musk of her quim filled with my essence. She massaged my head, face, and shoulders while chanting one of the holy incantations.

Her hands were charged with a static electricity that made my hair stand on end. She next massaged deeply my chest, so deep, I could feel her hands in me. My heart felt an ecstasy even greater than before as her hands gripped my heart.

She howled loudly as she pulled my heart out and held it up above me. It was still beating in her hands, dripping blood on my face. Her shrill cry matched the sound of the flute. There was nothing joyful about it, yet I remained serene.

I awoke to the shrilling wind of a rainstorm. The rainwater had found a leak in the roof and was dripping on my face. I clutched my beating heart, making sure it was still there. I looked around the morning gloom and felt reassured that the vision was over. I was surrounded by the usual empty loneliness. As I closed the front door behind me, I smiled and proceeded down the hill in the rain toward the sea.

CHAPTER SEVENTEEN

Approaching my grand, old, green, iron gate, I wondered if we would ever end my insecurity of when our next meeting would be. I never was sure when or even if we would meet again. That fact never helped my state of mind, which sometimes seemed to be ever more unhinged.

After entering my apartment, I absent-mindedly stuck my keys into my coat pocket. There I felt a folded note. I opened it. It was a note from her! I fell into the nearest chair and started to read it with dread, thinking she was finally calling it off. But no. It was the opposite.

My precious lover, the uncertainty of our next encounter must cause you much mental anguish. My driver will pick you up at your place next Wednesday at 2200. Yes, I know where you live. Do not ask how. I must force myself to concentrate on finishing all that I need to do as quickly as possible so we can run off together. That is what I want with all my heart. I believe you do, too.

All yours
Only After Dark

As my nervous tension turned to ecstatic joy, I realized how completely worn out I was. I took a hot shower, ate whatever I could find in the pantry, and had a long dreamless, restful nap. I awoke an hour later, much more refreshed. It was Monday. I had three days to fill, waiting for our next tryst.

I filled those days by taking long walks along the ocean on the Paredão with a serene mind. I had not felt so much at peace with the world, and most importantly with myself, in many years. I ate well and decided to limit my alcohol intake to only one bottle of wine a night. Earplugs were enough to help me sleep through the noisy nights of my invisible neighbors.

On Tuesday, I walked to the other side of Cascais to an important sight of the area. It was a large hollowed out rock formation that opened to the sea. Especially in the winter, the ocean waves would enter with such force that the water would crash five stories high up to the top. To many it appeared as an erupting volcano. It was originally a sea cave until the roof collapsed, leaving the center exposed to the sky.

Many cross-starred lovers were said to have jumped hand in hand to their deaths from the top, a Portuguese lover's leap. Many fishermen, casting their lines from the edge of the nearby cliffs, have been swept away by the occasional rogue waves. The locals call it Boca do Inferno, the Mouth of Hell.

Most people would visit for about ten minutes. I spent nearly ten hours there. The name, the drama of each crashing wave, the wild sea stretching far beyond the endless grey horizon, all of it captured my imagination.

I stood at the edge of the collapsed roof of the old sea cave, looking down at the sea nymphs gamboling in the waves below. I imagined how it would be to make that final leap into the watery abyss to let the nymphs take me to their hidden lairs and have their way with me.

With my eyes close and my arms outstretched, I wavered at the mouth of my imaginary doom. A strong arm grabbed my shoulder

Boca do Inferno

and pulled me away. It was the local gendarme and guard of the place. The meaning of his admonishment in Portuguese was clear to me. It was dangerous, and I was not supposed to be there. That is why there were guard rails which I obviously climbed over.

It was cold and already dark. I warmed myself at the local café for the fishermen with a meal of stewed gizzards and several glasses of aguardente. The café owner spoke some English and told me when the next bus would be back to town. He also mentioned that I should look to my left soon after the bus picked me up and notice the majestic palace of Umberto II, the last King of Italy, who still lived there.

I did as directed, and indeed the exceptionally large palace stood out in the darkness overlooking the Atlantic. It was in better shape than mine, but I thought it strange that except for a lone lit window at the top of the tower, it was completely dark everywhere else. The King of Italy was clearly better off than my poorer King of Romania, but probably just as lonely.

The abdicated King Edward VIII of the UK lived here a while. The deposed King Alfonso XIII of Spain lived a few blocks behind the palace of King Carlos II of Romania, where I lived. The Regent of Hungary and the royal pretenders to the thrones of France, Austria, and Spain (in the same town as the recognized King of Spain) lived here in exile. Even the deposed dictator Batista of Cuba landed here after Castro's Revolution, all managing to end their days in royal opulence.

From the Cascais bus station, I walked the rest of the way home along the Paredão. My mind gently drifted from one happy thought to another. I stopped to rest at my favorite bench, where only three weeks ago my beautiful love goddess came to me the first time.

Though we were to meet the next night, I decided to concentrate on her to see if she would appear beside me a night early. After twenty minutes, I realized it was hopeless. I was drawing a blank. Even her face refused to appear in my mind. I was empty. She was

The palace of King Umberto II, today a part of the Grande Real
Villa Italia Hotel.

not there. That was worrisome, but I knew I only had one more day until we would meet as she promised.

I stopped at my favorite neighborhood restaurant next to the Deck Bar to have a bottle of wine and some Portuguese petiscos to finish the evening. Both the restaurant and the bar were quite busy, even at 2230 in the evening. My favorite waiter from the Deck Bar strolled over.

"I haven't seen you in a while. How are things in the old palace?"

"Getting better. I've been fixing the place up. Found a new woman friend. We are getting along very well, exceedingly well, I must add."

"Good for you. Our Portuguese women like to please their men." He said with a wink.

"Yes, she is pleasing in every way. She and her family own many old mansions around Estoril."

"Ah, a rich and bored Portuguese woman. That's different. Be careful. Many of them become a femme fatale with their men. I believe your American expression is 'boy toys'. I love that expression."

"I can tell you she is no femme fatale, and I certainly am no boy toy."

"I'm just saying. I've seen a lot of these dramas play out right here. Only two months ago one of these rich older Estoril women and her boy toy had a big fight at that table next to yours. He was from the US, too, I seem to remember. She was tired of him, and he just couldn't let her go.

"They started out peacefully enough. But then he went from urgently pleading to aggressive shouting. She stayed calm the whole time. Finally, another young man came to the table, took her hand, and led her to his waiting car. Apparently, she had planned it that way.

"The American was left alone, sobbing uncontrollably. It was a sad sight to see a grown man wailing in public like a baby. He drank a bottle of aguardente and jumped in front of the Lisboa train right over there and killed himself."

"Sorry to hear that. But we're completely different. We're making plans for our future. Look, I don't want to talk about it. How is the local football team, the Estoril Praia, doing? When is their next game? The stadium is only about a fifteen-minute walk from my door." I changed the subject as anger was welling up in me, anger with one of the few friends I had here.

He shrugged his shoulders, wished me luck, and slouched back to the Deck Bar. I was seriously agitated, yet I could not explain to myself why the reaction. To calm down before returning home, I went to my favorite casino bar to find some distraction.

Of course, my other Estoril friend was holding court there, as he did almost every night. First, my irritation welled up again. Then I thought he could be entertaining and decided to give him a chance. I ordered a single malt scotch at the bar.

He noticed me with a brilliant grin. He told everyone around him that his American friend had arrived, and he had important things to discuss with me. They dispersed, and he motioned for me to sit next to him.

"Ah, my dear sir. How have you been? How are you and that love goddess of yours coming along?"

"We're doing great, but I don't think I would describe her as a 'love goddess'." I said with a huff, knowing full well that was exactly how I referred to her in my thoughts.

"Oh, come now. Nothing wrong with falling in love with a love goddess. That's every man's dream, isn't it?"

"Maybe for others, but not for me. I want a woman of maidenly flesh and hot blood." I lied, as that was exactly what I wanted, a love goddess to be sure.

"OK, fine, as you like. Tell me. It's been what, almost two weeks since we last met. Do you know anything more about her?"

"Not really. I don't ask about her past. I don't care about her former life or lives. I only care about our future together."

"So, you're getting married and having a family?"

"No. Well, not yet anyway. We'll live together and travel the world on her magnificent yacht."

"That sounds wonderfully romantic. What will be your first port of call?"

"We haven't discussed concrete plans yet. I think we'll do that when we meet again tomorrow night."

"Nice but listen to me," his voice sobered. "Think before you leap. In fact, whatever she proposes, come here and run it past me first. Seems to me you are not in your right mind to make serious decisions. Compared to the last time we met, you are much more infatuated with her. I'd say almost feverishly so. That's extremely dangerous for any man."

"Why is it that when one man tells another of his good fortune in finding the perfect woman, the other gets jealous and tries to throw cold water on it? God, it's irritating!"

"Friend, best to leave God out of it. Rather than invoke His name in exasperation, I think serious prayer would be a better idea in your case."

"Yes, let's leave God out of it. You can be sure that I will not tell you, God, or anyone else what my precious love goddess plans to do with me." My irritation was turning into anger as the alcohol was clouding my mind, winding my emotions up even higher than normal.

"What did you just say?"

"I meant what my beautiful lover and I plan to do together." I stammered my correction. "Of course, I am a grown man with much experience with women. If things don't work out and we break up, I can handle it. I won't jump in front of a train or anything."

I could barely put those thoughts to words, but I had to appear manly in presence of this odd person who was clearly winding me up. The fact was I had no idea how I would handle a breakup with her.

"Yes, please don't do anything drastic. After all, she's only a woman. Remember that. Unless she's not. Then that is another subject."

"I can assure you she is definitely a woman containing every part of a woman in the precisely correct place. What else could she be?"

"Do you want me to answer that or are you merely waxing rhetorically?"

"Oh, never mind. Let's change the subject. When is the next match of Estoril Praia? I really must see a game in their stadium. It's only about a fifteen-minute walk from here." I said, repeating my subject-changing tact I had used earlier with the Deck Bar waiter.

"You'd rather talk football? OK, fine. Bartender, another round for both of us."

CHAPTER EIGHTEEN

Charlie Parker's exuberant saxophone blared through my radio and woke me when the mellow classical music program of the night changed to bebop jazz. My head was in a bit of a haze from the night before. Reaching over to turn off the radio, I realized that there was something deep inside that bothered me to the point that I would try to drink enough to drive it out of my mind. I laid back and tried to pinpoint the source of this angst.

My thoughts were rambling and lost, but then a thread appeared. My mind followed that thread, pulling on it to see where it would lead. I abruptly stopped when I realized the more I pulled on the ephemeral thread of thought, the more I was unravelling the cerebral sweater that kept my mind warm and cozy. I dropped the thread when I realized that this was the night we would meet again.

A new dilemma presented itself. How was I to pass the next twelve hours? Much to my dismay, after doing my morning ablutions, preparing breakfast, and tidying up my small apartment only an hour had passed. While trying to concentrate on doing many little chores such as washing clothes, dishes, and the like, I checked my watch every ten minutes, willing the hour hand to move faster.

I gave up and decided to while away the hours walking along the churning sea. This time I decided to walk in the opposite direction of Cascais, toward Lisboa. After the Paredão ended, I continued on the narrow pathway beside the Marginal on the cliffs high above the crashing waves below. An hour later, I reached the long beach of Carcavelos. I found a café that was open in the winter and warmed myself with a double espresso and a hot snack by the coal-fired stove.

While watching the waves crash over the wharf, I asked for a pen and paper to write a poem. Focusing on the words flowing from the pen, I realized that I had a lot of passion built up in me. Unfortunately, my words were failing to capture how I was feeling.

First, I struggled to write lines in rhyme and meter. The structure was too much to bear. So, I dropped the rhyming. Counting out the syllables of each sentence proved impossible. I ended up just writing seemingly random phrases and words.

After a while, I struggled to make sense of it. I noticed a common thread tying them together: sex. I wrote about the sensation of being inside her, how her body would react when I touched her there, the primordial scent of our bodily fluids mixing together, her groans and growls, the beauty of her body described in multiple ways, etc. Between thoughts, I doodled in the margins erotic images of us in the act from various poses.

There was not one word regarding her astute mind, her wonderful personality, her sweet kindness. I realized that I knew almost nothing about her personality. Clearly our relationship was purely physical. But she had an animal magnetism that drew me to her like a moth to a flame.

Suddenly, a brief moment of lucidity cleared my mind. I decided we must share everyday all day together forever or I must break the whole thing off. I could not continue living 95% of my time alone in a confused near stupor, anxiously waiting for the remaining 5% in the heights of ecstasy.

As soon as I tried to imagine not having her at all, my entire being was thrown into a panic. I fell off my chair, landing with a sobering thud onto the floor. Embarrassed, I apologized and waved off the help of the waiter.

Many sheets of paper and hours later I sought to arrange these random words and phrases born from my stream of consciousness into what could pass for a poem. It was nothing but feverish scribble with much of it crossed out. I crumpled all the pages into tightly wound balls and threw them out. I looked at my watch. Happily, I noticed that the afternoon would be gone by the time I returned to my lair.

Slowly, I walked back to Estoril. The realization slowly dawned on me that I had lost control of my life. Fortunately, I was a successful writer with money in the bank, I had the luxury of allowing myself to fall into such a trap where I found myself.

If I had to go to work every day and concentrate on a job, I probably would have been fired by now. The fact that my words so spectacularly failed to express my direct feelings in a short poem meant it would be hopeless to embark on a new novel.

By the time my feet found their way back to the Estoril train station, where I would pass under the tunnel to the expansive casino park on the other side, I realized that I was clearly in uncharted territory. My mind was exhausted from flipping between anxiety of my mental state and the thrill of knowing that in a few hours I would be in the arms of my Only After Dark.

The memory of her beautiful, warm, soft, maidenly body entwining mine with her heavenly passionate embrace, her heavy full breasts smothering me with her love, the perfume of her long hair hanging down, completely embracing my head and face quickened my pace. I instinctively looked at my watch, only to be disappointed by how much time I still had.

As I passed the Deck Bar, my favorite waiter stood in the doorway and gave me a double thumbs up with a beaming smile. I did the same back to him. I wondered what he meant by it, but concluded he was just sharing the universal happiness that I was experiencing. What else could it have meant?

But then I remembered that everyone I had passed smiled at me. Were they merely being warmly friendly toward a fellow pedestrian taking a walk in the damp winter cold? Or could they see my happiness beaming from my face and that brought a smile to their faces, too? Or maybe they knew something I did not? Was there a colossal, secret, universal joke at my expense that somehow escaped me?

I pulled back from this darkening train of thought. After all, a smile was not the same as a smirk, a chuckle, or even an outright guffaw. I settled on when we are happy, all the world is our friend, instinctively wanting to share a happiness that binds us all together. Thinking of the approaching evening darkness, I could barely keep my feet on the ground. My entire being just wanted to float the rest of the way home.

Back in my apartment, I made a cup of tea and ate whatever I could scrounge up, knowing that I would have a sumptuous feast later. I chose to warm myself with a hot bath. As the hot water filled the large bathtub, I stood nude in front of the wall mirror in the bathroom.

I was surprised that despite all those feasts and my excessive drinking, I was losing a lot of weight. In fact, I had to admit I was looking rather good. I concluded it was due to all the walking and lovemaking I was doing. That last thought brought a smile to my face, and I slipped into the steamy bath.

Lost in revelry, my thoughts wandered. I imagined myself living and breathing underwater. There was an entire city under the ocean, populated with sea maiden nymphs. I was Poseidon, the great god-king of the sea, the equal of Zeus. My subjects, all the denizens of the deep, were so eager to serve me, to please me.

Standing on the veranda of my underwater palace, I looked out over my city with its fantastic exotic minarets in every hue and color. It reminded me of something that Dr. Seuss would have designed. My subjects floated among the crenellated towers at all levels, as they were not limited to walking on the ground. They were all weightless as birds resting with wings outstretched on an air current from a mountain breeze.

My Aphrodite was standing beside me the whole time, a consort fit for a god. She was holding my hand, smiling at me every moment I looked upon her radiant face. Her smile was not of desire and lust, but rather of a divine love and devotion. I basked in the warmth of my newfound happiness and contentment. I discovered my life-mate.

Our city was not so far below the water's surface. The sun in the blue sky above illuminated our metropolis in a pure light. I clapped my hands for my chariot pulled by dolphins. I took the reins and drew her next to me. I showed her all the wonders of my underwater world gliding below us.

She asked for the reigns. I let her take us to wherever her heart desired. The dolphins pulled us tirelessly. Their undulating tales in front of us never slowed. Eventually, we came to the foot of a long range of cliffs. We continued along the cliff base until a large, dark entrance of a sea cave appeared. She directed the dolphins inside. Darkness enveloped us the deeper into the cave we went. My proud confidence was turning into fear. Where was she taking us with such determination?

My dream was interrupted by an eerie shrieking, like a specter would do in a B-rated horror movie. My eyes suddenly opened, and the shriek stopped. Confusion filled my mind when I noticed that the hot steamy air had turned into a clammy dampness and my bath water had become cold. Panic quickly followed when I realized I had fallen asleep. What time was it?

I reached for my watch. Relief filled me when I realized I had less than an hour until her chauffeur would pick me up. I shaved, perfumed myself, and put on the best clothes I brought with me. I paced back and forth, excited that I would soon be with my love. I recognized that I was not just infatuated with her, but completely obsessed with her. I calmed myself by considering that everything would be fine once we could spend every day together. It was being apart that so unhinged me.

Finally, I could take it no more. I stood outside my gate in the cold with still fifteen minutes to go, thinking the driver might come early. My eyes looked in every direction down the palely lit streets, having no idea from what direction he would come.

Impatience welled up in my heart as it was a quarter past ten and he still had not arrived. I laughed at myself for assuming that he would arrive early. This was southern Europe, after all. Nothing ever happened on time. Whenever the occasional car passed, my mind bounced like a yo-yo. Was this the one or not?

At twenty-five minutes past the hour, her Bentley stopped in front of me. The chauffeur leapt out and quickly opened the back door. I collapsed onto the rich plush leather seat, exhausted by the tormenting day of waiting. I quickly perked up, hoping the next derelict mansion we approached would be hers.

For twenty minutes, the car carried us ever higher and further from the sea. We were in the forest now. I tried to follow the way we took so I might find my way back the next morning. I gave up. Finally, the car stopped in front of an old iron gate. The chauffeur opened it and we slowly drove up a driveway to a castle sitting in a clearing on the hilltop.

Its single tall tower soared high above the trees. The dark clouds occasionally opened a space for the moon to light our path, mingling with the shadows of forest and tower together. In the dark distance, a dog howled balefully. When the moon retreated, everything went black except for a dull light glimmering from the open front door. There she was, framed by the warm glow behind her, waiting for me in her shimmering rainbow-colored robe. My heart leapt with joy.

Her house where the Grand Ball was held 45 years ago.

CHAPTER NINETEEN

As I started walking towards her, a chill gripped me. It was not the chill of the biting wind, all the stronger for being higher up the hill. No, it was a chill from within, coming from deep inside me, a chill of dread. It was an irrational feeling, probably caused by the eerie places where we always met. There was nothing normal about anything with us.

She beckoned me to her. "Come on, silly! What are you waiting for?"

Her voice drove far away all doubts and chills. My feet quickened their pace as my heart quickened its beat at the sound of her mellifluous voice. When we were at arm's reach, she reached out and pulled me to her like iron to a magnet. As she kissed my neck, a wave of warmth spread throughout me, replacing doubts with certainty.

She pulled me inside and shut the winter's frigid breath out behind us. She undressed me in the foyer and clothed me with my matching feather robe. She took my hand, holding it high at shoulder height as if we were starting a renaissance dance, and led me into the main room. The warmth of the house surprised me. The heat and bright light were not coming from only a fireplace and candles.

We left a winter's midnight and entered a summer's midday. Instead of the normal living room with a dining table and a bed fitted in the corner, before me was a vast hall. The dining table stretched far towards the opposite wall, with place settings for forty. The ceiling was just visible high above where the moonlight barely revealed a color glass ceiling, a mosaic of rich blues, reds, and greens.

Several great crystal chandeliers hanging down from high above illuminated every corner with a dazzling brightness. The light nearly blinded me as if I looked directly into the sun at noon. It was not only light these little suns produced but also the warmth of a mother's arms, a warmth that filled the heart.

The walls were covered in paintings of harlequins with bells and colorful attire, reminding me of a Venetian festival. A fireplace roared with fierce flames, adding its own heat and brightness. The space between it and the dominant dining table was large enough for a ball. And a ball there was.

We were not alone. Eight musicians stood to the side playing renaissance music on their lutes, recorders, guitars, and kettle drums. Dozens danced a highly formalized but lascivious ritual. Servers holding laden silver trays stood at a respectable distance to the sides.

Everyone wore carnival masks of either Comedy or Tragedy of classical Greek times. The Comedy masks were caricatures of the hilarity of madness, with smiles bordering on grimaces. The Tragedy masks were faces at the height of sorrowful angst. Just showing below the masks, men and women alike, were their heavily rouged pouting lips, begging to be kissed.

What most startled me was everybody was nude. Their bodies unashamedly crossed the full spectrum, from the firmness of youth to the gravity heavy bodies of old age. There were tall ones, short ones, tautly thin to morbidly obese, and bodies of every color. There were breasts of every kind: tightly defined muscular ones, proudly pert ones with the blush of youth, fully laden mature ones. I was especially intrigued that below the shoulders everyone was hairless.

"Come. Let's have a glass of wine by the fireplace and watch the dance." She motioned over to one of the servers who was holding a tray of generously poured crimson-colored glasses.

Speechless, all I could do was follow her with glass in hand. After a few gulps of calming liquid, I found my voice. "What is this?"

"It's a special gift for you. Think of it as a surprise party. I can see you are surprised. It worked!" She said with a girlish giggle.

"You certainly did!" The wine, the bodies, and the suggestive dancing were having their effect on me.

She purred in my ear, "Hm, I notice you are posting to the right. So, you like what you see, no? These are all my especially close friends. If any of them catches your eye, man or woman, I wish you to take them in the next room. In fact, I urge you to. It would please me greatly."

"N-n-no. I-I only have eyes for you." I stammered, surprised at her swinging attitude toward sex. "I only desire you. You are perfect for me, perfect in every way."

"Well, then, I guess you will have to take me. And I do mean 'take me'. I am yours no matter if you want to share your manliness with others. I've never experienced such pleasure as I have with you. But shall we dine first?"

I nodded, trying to digest what I just heard. She clapped her hands loudly like a sultan signaling his slaves. "Shall we?" she called, motioning to the table.

Everyone stopped in mid-motion, in mid-note, and sauntered to their designated places. She sat me at the head of the table with her to my right. In front of each of us were a stack of plates of different sizes with various sized utensils spreading to the left and right of the plates. We all had glasses already full of strong rich Douro wine at their proper places.

She stood up with glass in hand and announced, "I want to propose a toast. Everyone, this is my mate, my man. I have chosen him above all others to be by my side forever. As my dear friends, you know what this means to me, how important he is to me and my life. Let's welcome him!" Everybody stood with their glasses held outstretched and gave me a warm welcome, with cries of emotional platitudes.

The servers started to serve the nine-course meal. The table erupted in riotous conversation as everyone turned to their neighbors, leaving us to each other. She turned to me.

"I know something is bothering you, my precious." she said, leaning close to me. "I realize because of my hectic and ever-changing schedule; we have not been able to plan precisely the next time we meet. That must cause you a lot of uncertainty. From now on, we will plan every encounter together. Would you like that?"

"Oh, yes, I would like that very much. Of course, I understand you are far busier than I am, but still, it would free my mind from wondering if you would appear while I sit on the frigid bench by the sea."

"Fine. Before this evening is over, we will have a precise place and time for our next time together. How do you like everything so far?"

"Everything is perfectly wonderful as always, my love."

We chattered throughout the dinner. Well, in fact, I did most of the chattering. She answered my questions about her with questions about me. When it came to talking about herself, her answers were always vague and cryptic. She was exactly as mysterious as the first night we met. I decided that was just all right with me. The past did not matter. Only the present and every present moment into the future.

I will not bore you by describing the details of our five-star Michelin dinner. As our nude company was relaxing with their glasses of port wine, she whispered in my ear, "It's time, my man. Lead me to the next room, through the red door. I want you. I want to feel you inside me."

Leaping up, nearly knocking over my chair, I took her by the hand and led her purposely towards the crimson red door. Everyone stopped their conversations and cheered us with whistles and applause, like we were at a sporting event. I was ready to perform at my peak.

Opening the door, my eyes had to adjust to the darkness compared to the brilliance behind me. Concentric circles of musk-scented candles surrounded the familiar fountain standing erect in the center of its pool of warm water. Two young maidens stood by nude, waiting to serve as needed. Only After Dark removed our robes and handed one to each of them to hold for us.

She took vermillion powder from a brass bowl and tossed it into the water, producing a strong rose fragrance. Then she entered the pool. I needed no encouragement to follow her. I took her in my arms. She murmured in her husky voice, "Would you prefer them instead? I would greatly enjoy watching you give pleasure to others."

"No, my sweet. You are the only woman for me. Besides, I wouldn't want to share you with another man."

"Who said anything about me? I have no interest in any other man. I admit I occasionally enjoy a womanly touch. But I would never consider any man but you. So, are you sure?"

"Yes. I'm very sure."

"We'll see about that. Come to me. Come closer."

With her passionate kiss that nearly lit me on fire, we quickly started making love. I always marveled how she was always ready for me. She whispered into my ear a strange question that switched my gears from physical to mental. "Please don't think too much before answering. Can you promise me you will answer from your heart, the first thing that comes to mind? Can you?"

In the throes of passion, my mind could not focus on counting to ten if it had to. I answered, "Sure. What is it?"

"Do I have your soul?"

But this question bored into my conscience, stopping me in mid-stream. "My soul?"

"Yes. Your soul. Don't worry. I'm not the Devil in disguise. I just want to know if I have you completely. Are you the one I will spend all eternity together pleasing him in every way? Are you the one? Consider it merely a metaphorical question."

A metaphorical question? I asked myself. *How can women in the midst of passionate love making stop and ask a metaphorical question?* Since the blood of my brain had mostly drained to my smaller head, all I could do was follow her instructions and answer the first thing that came to mind.

My passion answered for me, "Yes, of course, my love! You have me completely, in every way possible."

"Excellent." She continued her rocking motion on me.

We tried several positions but as usual we always ended with her straddling my lap, bobbing up and down with her beautiful full maidenly breasts cradling my face. At last, she clenched my head tightly into her breasts and with a loud shriek came to orgasm, signaling me to do the same. I unclenched my eyes and noticed the two maidens smiling with approval. I agreed. We did extraordinarily well together.

When our heartbeats slowed enough to catch our breath to speak, she whispered softly, "I've made up my mind about you, my precious. Today is Wednesday. I have just a few things to finish. Let's meet Friday night at our usual hour on the Paredão, but not at our bench. We'll meet at the end of the wharf next to it. You know, where the stone pillar is.

"I want to show you something special. It's time I consider about us and stop all my ridiculous family affairs. My family can take care of itself. I have way more than enough money to keep us in great comfort forever."

I held her tightly against me and murmured my reply, "Wonderful! I'll be there."

"Good. Now that we have that settled, let's not keep our goddess waiting."

We rose and the two maidens-in-waiting gently toweled us dry and clothed us in our robes. Hand in hand, we returned to the main room. In the center of the previous dance floor was our vulpine love goddess. Our dinner guests were all kneeling, still in the nude, in concentric circles around her. Before her was a mattress that was our place to kneel below her outstretched arms, as if embracing her lover. Wafting in the air was a strange but pleasing incense of something between camphor and eucalyptus.

Everyone started the familiar chanting. For the first time I joined in chanting the strange and unknown language. It was the same as before: 'wamba bam bami bam mi bam shamma lamma oo mao mao shuga dido'. At least that is what it sounded like to me. My mind relaxed with my body into the warmth of our voices intoning together. We chanted this for nearly half an hour until we concluded with a loud 'Aohommmm'.

We knelt in silence. I marveled at my sudden state of liberation. All inhibitions and cares dropped from my shoulders as if I removed a heavy backpack. I knew I made the right decision. As if she understood my thoughts, she clasped my hand, smiling benevolently.

She rose and removed both of our robes, becoming nude like everyone else. She laid me on the mattress, stretched out on my back. She kneeled beside me and surprised me with a strange question.

"It's time for you to greet our friends. They are eager to introduce themselves to you. Would you prefer to greet our girlfriends, our boyfriends, or both?"

"Both? No, I would much prefer to meet our girlfriends. I just don't swing any other way."

"As you prefer. Think of this as sharing the chalice of wine, the chalice of communion. And you, my precious love, are the chalice. I want you to close your eyes and relax."

I did as she instructed, with no idea what she meant. She orally aroused me again. In such a state, one by one the women in the room mounted me for about thirty seconds, murmuring their names in my ear. At the end, when I could take it no more, the familiar musky smell of my Only After Dark filled my senses, letting me know who finished me off.

She helped me sit up and raised as an offering high above her head a communion chalice, a chalice of gold and gems, perhaps an ancient holy grail. The fragrance rising from the chalice reminded me of an ancient port wine, but even more pungent and enticing. I drank the whole cup in a long single gulp. Everything started to spin around me. The once bright light dimmed until darkness. I laid back in ecstasy.

I was standing alone in the usual jungle clearing of my dreams. The strange gate held my attention. There was a terrible light seeping out through whatever crack it could find. The hum of our votive chanting came from behind the door.

An invisible hand rapped the great brass knocker. Suddenly, the door swung open and individual points of light rushed forth like spirits escaping from the terrible maw of hell. Each one found a bit of darkness and illuminated it until the jungle disappeared into an intense blinding white light.

Inside the doorway became pitch black, with not a speck of light. Out of the all-consuming darkness stepped my fox spirit. She stood in front of the gate with her arms held out to me like the statue. She continued the familiar chant and with her hands beckoned me to her bosom. My heart filled with delirious yearning. I stepped forward towards her calming embrace, my haven, my sanctuary. That was the last thing I remembered.

CHAPTER TWENTY

The next morning, I awoke, resigned to being alone again. And I was, but incredibly, I was lying in my own bed. I was disoriented as I tried to remember what happened the night before. I pieced together everything until the moment I passed out. How did I end up back in my bed? Was it all a dream? How disappointing that would be!

I turned over to see the time and on the side table was a note and my keys beside it. I grabbed the note. It read: **Dearest love, we brought you home and put you to sleep. Hope you have a great day tomorrow. Remember! Only one more day until we meet again! We will leave this place soon. Until then, all of my love.**

Only After Dark.

I was relieved it was not a dream. But now I only had a day and a half until our next meeting. How to fill the time? Since I had a specific hour and place for our next encounter, I was relaxed about it, almost serene. I laid back on my pillow and remembered all the pleasures and bizarreness of the night before. What a night! It was as incredible as it was strange. Everything about it was a fantasy that came true. It thoroughly wore me out. My eyes slowly closed, and I fell back to sleep.

Two hours later, I awoke, surprisingly refreshed and well rested, considering all the excesses of the lascivious ball from the previous night. I threw off the covers and decided it was time to start my day. It was still before noon. I had time to actually accomplish something. But what? Yesterday was market day, so I missed that. The shining sun invited me out of my dark lair. I would go for a walk. I brought my notebook and pen in my knapsack.

Perhaps I would write my poem or even the outline of my next novel. For the first time since I arrived, I felt I could concentrate on something besides the pain I was running from. Instead, my new destination was the newfound passion and happiness that filled my every fiber.

The Paredão and its view of the sea was as inviting as ever. The winter sea had a rare calm. The barely audible rhythm of the waves lapping the rocks below brought a peace I had not felt for many years. The tension of my mind and body dissolved away like a rain puddle on a sunny day. The voices of the seagulls above me were music, music of the gods. I stopped and leaned on a railing, admiring the harbor and the silhouette of Cascais in the distance.

I fell into a revelry, almost a meditation with, instead of a Mandela in front of me, the stunning view across the bend in the coast of Cascais and its colorful fishing boats bobbing in the harbor. A dog sniffing at my leg interrupted my serenity. It started to alternatively bark and growl at me. Why was that stupid creature bothering me? Was the wretched cur trying to communicate something to me? Did it sense something threatening about me?

Its owner called it back to him. Reluctantly, it turned and retreated. Normally, that would have ruined my day, but I was in too good a mood to let petty things bother me. Broken from my trance, I continued to Cascais. I found my way to my favorite nuts and berries shop. I bought a mixture of both and would reach into the paper bag for a handful every few minutes as I continued my stroll. My next stop was the city library. Maybe the librarian had some news for me, though in truth it no longer really mattered.

The assistant librarian greeted me warmly. She told me that her boss called and told her she found a most fascinating discovery regarding my request. She would be back the next Monday. I should return that afternoon for a debriefing. I thanked her and continued to my favorite cafe across from the city lighthouse where I ordered a hot lunch of marinated chicken gizzards with a mug of Super Bock lager, which, if you do not mind, I prefer to the only other choice of Sagres.

After finishing lunch, I pulled out my notebook and stared at the clean blank page for a few minutes. Then, with a newly found clarity of mind, I purposely wrote a detailed outline of my next novel. It would be very autobiographical. Its working title was 'Only After Dark'. In fact, the novel would be an account of what I had experienced from my near mental breakdown at the hands of my nasty, cheating, ex-wife to my current thrilling heights of bliss.

Scribbling my detailed outline took me almost to the end of the afternoon. Thousands of words described in broad brush strokes my strange adventures. But how to finish it? What would be the conclusion of all this? I did not want it to be a diary of our adventures together that I kept for the next forty years. No, it was to be my next bestseller.

A few hours later as the sun sank in the western ocean, I decided the story would conclude with us living on her yacht sailing the ocean blue, finding adventures all around the world. So, I wrote at the bottom of the last page: "Then we sailed off into the broad moonlight. The End." The satisfaction of setting in motion my next great work brought a warm sense of accomplishment and a broad smile on my face.

I was energized, even ecstatic, as I left the restaurant. I decided to stop by and say hello to the few people I met since my arrival. The first stop was the concierge at the Hotel Baia where I stayed when I first arrived. I stopped by and chatted with the young salesman who sold me my boombox radio and music player. They were glad to see me and noted that Portugal apparently was treating me well by the radiant glow beaming from me. I had to agree that indeed it was treating me wonderfully.

Finally, I made my way to the Deck Bar back in Estoril. It was time for dinner, anyway. I sat outside under the great canopy of the serene tree branches spreading their sheltering arms above me and enjoyed the cool sea breeze. My favorite waiter was there as usual. He gave me a great hug, greeting me warmly. He brought me their best wine and the dish of the day.

I related everything that had happened since we last spoke.

He replied, "I'm so happy for you. It appears that coming to Estoril was a great idea."

"Yes, it was one of the best decisions I've ever made."

"As for me," he sighed, "my life is still the same as it has been for the past twenty-six years. I admit sometimes to myself that my life is boring: being a waiter with little prospects of anything better, married to a woman I neither love, yet has given me little reason to complain as wives go, having very normal but dull children, who probably will never amount to much more than me."

All I could respond to that list of misery was, "Never give up. Stay open to any new adventures that may come your way."

He laughed at my advice. "No adventures for me. No thanks. Being open to 'new adventures' most likely would lead to disaster. The best I or anyone else can do is accept our lot in life and find comfort in the small things."

I countered, "Perhaps for most 'normal' people, but I'm a dreamer. As such, I prefer a life of adventures no matter how much sorrow they might bring me in the end, rather than a boring banal empty life."

"No, I never dream of anything other than getting through life, with the least sorrow as possible. If I don't dream, I won't be disappointed."

"Well, I guess we can't all be dreamers," came my weak reply.

"No, my friend. But I'm happy to meet at least one dreamer. You keep dreaming for the rest of us." And he sauntered away with an air of sorrow and his familiar slouch.

His bleak summary of life saddened me. Yet, it did accurately capture the state of mind of nearly all people around the world. I shrugged my shoulders, as if to shake off his cloak of despair, and started on my savory dinner and a bottle of Alentejan wine.

Since I was still worn out from the night before, I went to bed early regardless of the normal shrieking. Back in my home, I was about to turn my radio on to drown out the infernal noises of the night. when I realized, for the first time since I moved in, there was only silence. I opened my door and walked down the empty dark hall, just to be certain. The silence was even more eerie than the ghastly cries.

I calmly accepted the change as I had accepted everything else that was happening to me and slept soundly the whole night through. My dreams were as empty as the silence pervading my decrepit palace. The silence continued to the morning when even the birds were silent in the garden grounds outside my windows. Did I lose my hearing? The sound of my hands clapping reassured me.

The thought that I was to meet my precious Only After Dark that very night put me in an ecstatic mood. I was so excited that I could not sit down. I paced through the salons, eating my egg custard tarts, and spilling my coffee on my hand.

I tried to sit at my desk and put the initial layer of flesh on the outline I created the previous day for my next novel. It was too difficult to focus my thoughts.

I found myself easily distracted and tapping out some kind of morse code message on the desk with my pen. It sounded like the morse code from the old movies. Was it 'Mayday' or 'Save Our Ship'? I could never remember.

Many hours later, I finished the first patina of detail. I reread my work as I paced in circles around my apartment until the late afternoon sun started fading.

About halfway through, I stopped in mid-step. It occurred to me I was merely repeating the details of what happened rather than a fictional account of a bizarre relationship that no one could have invented, not even me. But there it was, a diary of strangeness. It was absolutely incredible what I had been through and what I was in the midst of. Reading it as a novel dispassionately made me think it must be too good to be true. Was it?

That doubt was doused as a strong yearning grew in my heart for the touch of her soft breasts brushing across my face as her body gripped mine so tightly, I could barely move. I reveled in the memory of our shared experiences until I noticed I was aroused. It was too early for that. To distract my amorous thoughts, I walked through the dingy halls. Maybe I would meet the crazy old man who lived upstairs.

CHAPTER TWENTY-ONE

The eerie gloom and the old creaking floorboards of the corridor bowed a little under my feet as I walked past the strange, locked doors hiding who knows what secrets. I asked myself why I strangely felt compelled to visit everyone I met in Portugal before my rendezvous later with her. I had a premonition that I might be leaving that night. How or where, I could not say.

My steps led me to his door, which was surprisingly open. I did not notice before that his door was made of thick iron with steel pegs running down the edge that would insert themselves into the door frame when locked like a bank vault. It had a veneer of wood on the outside identical to all the other doors down the hall.

I knocked on the open door and peered inside. There he was preparing something at his desk with many small parts. I must have startled him, as he gave a yelp and dropped what he was holding. He turned around with fear in his eyes.

"Calm down, my old friend. It's just me. Thought I would drop by and see how you're doing."

"Oh, it's you. I heard you were leaving us or already had left us."

"Leave? Whoever or whatever gave you that idea?"

"The property manager told me."

"He communicated with you? I never told him anything of the sort. I may go on a trip soon, but I intend this to be my home, or at least the place where I put my things."

"Well, we shall see, won't we? We shall see."

"You talk as if I have no say in the matter."

"Often times in life we don't. We are often the passive playthings of life and her actors."

"Maybe so, but what about you?"

"Me? I'm the same. I will always be the same. It's too late for me to change now. I bet if you meet me in a thousand years, I'll be the same even then. I could have said 'forever', but that's a mighty long time. Forever could end tomorrow, a million years from now, or never."

"I have a different timeframe. I live day to day, open to whatever adventure comes my way."

"Ah, so you are leaving us."

"It's possible, I suppose, but it's not at all certain. I guess it depends on what happens tonight."

"Let me give you this advice, youngster. Cool it down. Get control of yourself. Trust me, you are in way over your head."

"How do you know anything about my situation?"

"It's been broadcasted to the heavens, my boy. Everyone knows about it. Well, everyone who counts, that is."

"Have you been talking to that guy at the casino bar?"

"No. I haven't stepped into a casino for over thirty years. I don't need to talk to anyone. I just know things."

"Know things? You know nothing about me, old man. I have plans. We have plans. I am in complete control of my life."

"Oh, really? Plans are abstract mind games. You aren't in control of anything. You can't control what will happen in the next five minutes, let alone in the next fifty years. Take my advice or not. It's your choice. We always have choices. At least there's always that."

"You know what? I regret coming up here to visit you. I don't understand how you think you know anything about me, but I can simply tell you that you're wrong about everything. I think it's best I leave now."

"Regret? You should rejoice. Either way, it's your decision. I wish you well on your journey though I am certain it won't end well."

With that last remark, I abruptly turned and left. Muttering angrily to myself all the way back, I was surprised how the old fool's words had such a powerful effect on me. I was determined not to let anything change the electric current running up and down my spine, nor the warm grip squeezing my heart. I had never felt so excited about meeting a woman ever. Not even for my first one, when my heart was full more of trepidation than desire.

I distracted myself by busily straightening up my place. I laid everything out to make it easier to pack up, if that was what the night would dictate. After I could do no more, I decided to eat dinner early and stop by the casino bar to distract myself until it was time. I could not bear to be in the same building as that crazy old coot upstairs.

The Deck Bar's jolly waiter would brighten my mood. I took a seat in the early evening's dying light. My favorite waiter was on his day off. That bothered me even more, though I cannot really explain why. He deserved a day off, many days off, in fact. I had a pleasant dinner with a bottle of their special wine. I prolonged dinner with a few glasses of port wine.

I crossed the street and walked through the casino's garden to the wood-paneled old world bar upstairs. There, my strange acquaintance was as well ensconced at the bar as usual. He rose and greeted me warmly with a hug and pulled me to the stool next to him.

"Well, you look wonderful. You're practically beaming. I guess things are going swimmingly with your love goddess."

"Yes. Yes, they are going swimmingly, as you put it. We will meet in a few hours again."

"Did you ever learn any more about her? Or about the strange rituals you described to me?"

"I asked the librarian at the Cascais library to research the sect or cult or whatever it is. She told me she would do so during her vacation at the University of Coimbra, which is in her hometown. She returns on Monday. I'll visit her then to understand better. But the fact is I don't really care anymore. It would only be intellectual curiosity at this point."

"Intellectual curiosity? I suggest you wait until you hear the librarian's report before you meet your love interest again. Don't you think it's important to understand what they believe in and what their end goals are? For all you know, it may be a vampire cult."

"Vampire cult? Now you're being ridiculous."

"Don't know about that. Though it does seem strange that you meet only after dark, don't you think? That's when they're active, right?"

"Look, we've been together for a few weeks now and there are no fang marks on me anywhere."

"Maybe it's not blood she is draining from you."

"That's absurd. Whatever precious bodily fluid I give her is completely voluntary. Can we talk about something else?"

"Fine. Fine. What about her? You must have learned more about her during this time."

"Her origins come from all across Europe. She's had several failed relationships before. Seems there was an ex-husband along the way. No children that I know of. She never mentions them if she has any. Her family is from old money, owns a lot of real estate in Estoril and probably many other places, too. She appears to be in her late thirties or early forties.

"That's about it. Not much, I understand, but if she wants to forget her past and start over with a clean slate, that's fine with me. I have my own past that I want to forget, a past that pains me even now to think about it."

"Well, that's not much, I agree. What about the cult? Have you experienced any more with that?"

"Up until two nights ago, it had always been just the two of us. But Wednesday we met at a large estate higher up the hills. There had to have been at least fifty people there, about half men and half women. It was a kind of masked ball with everyone in the nude. So, it's not only her, well, and me in it, whatever 'it' is."

"Oh, do go on."

"She seems very liberal with sex. She encourages me to have sex with other women or even men. She herself is not interested in other men. Not sure about women, though. In fact, for the grand finale of the evening she laid me down in front of the fox goddess and… I think that's enough detail."

"Come on! Tell me. You can't leave me hanging. How did it end?"

After all the wine, the port, and now my third scotch, my general contentment with my new life bubbled forth and made me speak of things I would normally never tell anyone. So, I continued.

"She told me the other adherents wanted to introduce themselves to me and would I prefer women or men or both. I made it clear to her I don't swing that way. I only am interested in women. I mentioned that as a point of fact, not as an answer to her strange question.

"As I was saying, she laid me down on my back in front of the smiling fox goddess statue. One by one, the other women mounted me for around a half a minute each. There were nearly two dozen of them in all shapes, sizes, and even ages. At the end of it all, she gave me a chalice of rich, musky wine. The next thing I remember was waking up to the morning light in my own bed. That's it really."

"Oh, my, God! That is incredible. I've heard of swinging parties, but nothing like that. You have certainly found yourself an incredibly special woman. What are your plans now?"

"Like I said, we are meeting later this evening, which reminds me I feel I've had enough to drink already. My head is spinning a bit. I think she wants to sail off into the moonlight with me on her yacht to travel the world and live happily ever after."

"That is a most amazing fantasy. A fantasy any man would love to experience. Good for you, my friend. I honestly am happy for you. Perhaps you can put in a kind word for me and let me join this cult."

"Sure, I could do that. You know what? I really do need some fresh air. So, I'll take my leave and see you soon." I rose a bit unsteadily from my bar stool.

He rose, too, and held my shoulders. "Are you sure you're all right? Do you want me to help you get home? Call a taxi?"

"No, no, I'm fine. I can't go home now. I need to meet my Only After Dark soon." I waved him off with a shaky flick of my hand.

"If you say so. I wish you the best of luck. As they say in Portugal, 'um abraço' which means 'one hug' in English." He gave me a tight hug that made me feel queasy. I smiled wanly and left. I needed to walk in the cold night air to help clear my cloudy head.

Back in the casino garden, my watch told me I had about a half an hour before our rendezvous. I slowly walked unevenly down the slope, through the tunnel, to the ocean on the other side. I took my shoes off and walked across the wide sandy beach to the long jetty, with the stone pillar at the end. The pillar reminded me of the pillory posts in the plazas of old European towns.

The sea was rough with waves crashing against the jetty, splashing frigid foamy water on my feet. That was exactly what I needed to sober up. I was a little early, so I breathed deeply the salty sea air into my lungs and enjoyed the lights of Cascais in the distance.

My heart leapt when the outline of a large two-masted ketch close to twenty meters (sixty-five feet) long appeared out of the darkness. It was barely visible because of the black sails and ultramarine colored hull in the moonless night. But the green light on the left and the red light on the right meant it was coming straight towards me. The small mast lights above twinkled like bobbing stars.

The pillar where they were to meet.

It was her! This was her wonderful plan. I knew it! She stopped about fifty meters (fifty-five yards) from me. Her melodious voice spoke to me through a megaphone.

"Dearest, it's so wonderful to see you! I decided that we leave tonight to start our journey together, a journey through place and time. I am so excited. Look, I thought I could dock at this jetty, but the tide is too low and there are rocks all around here. Go pack your things and let's meet at the Cascais marina in about an hour. I can dock there. There is a bar across from the public slip. I'll meet you there. My driver will pick you up at your place to bring you to me."

"No need, my precious," I shouted back as loud as I could. "I don't need anything else but you. I'm an excellent swimmer. I'll swim to you now." Before she could object, I dropped my coat and shoes on the ground and leapt into the heaving sea.

And that, my friend, is my story and I'm going to stick to it. Thank you for being so patient with me rambling on about my experiences since I arrived in Portugal. I feel it's somehow important that I relate my story to someone. I noticed you sitting tonight on this same bench where I started my adventure. So, I chose you to be the one to remember me.

When I first sat here on this very bench, I admit my mind was in turmoil from my nasty divorce, from the love of my life. So, I was alone here and open to whatever adventure that would present itself. But you're Portuguese. You have all your circles of family and friends. Are you sitting here hoping your love goddess would appear?

No? Just had a fight with your wife. I don't have any advice on that subject. There was a time when I would have given it freely, but now I'm in no position to advise anyone about anything. All I can say is I hope you get over your conflicts and not run away like I did.

Why am I all wet? That's simple. I've been swimming. You know, I'm an excellent swimmer. My wet clothes don't weigh me down and I don't feel the cold anymore. I must have become used to it. I swim like a sea sprite now.

Once I finish our conversation, I'll go back to swimming again. I need to reach her yacht. She is waiting for me, so we can start our voyage together. It's frustrating because I swim every night until the dawn, but I can never quite reach her. The waves and the tides take great delight in pushing her away from me every time I ever get close. But I will never give up! Do you understand? Even if it takes me an eternity! I must not disappoint her!

Look! That's her yacht over there. What do you mean you don't see anything? It's right there! You can see the little lights high on the masts and there's the port side red light. Did you hear that? She's calling for me. I really must get going. Do you have anything more to say before I take my leave?

What? You think I'm crazy? That's impossible. How could I be crazy with such a logical mind?

EPILOGUE

Special Investigator Rui Cunha Oliveira sat back in his desk chair and stared at the peeling paint on his office ceiling. His head was still in a fog from his usual nightly bottle of gin. After many years, his face showed the permanently haggard look and soulless eyes of a functioning alcoholic. Gin was his preferred method to self-medicate away the horrors he had witnessed and, worse, perpetrated as a commanding officer in the Special Operations arm of the counter-insurgency forces in Guinea-Bissau from only a few years before.

The open windows let in the fragrant Spring air, the rays of the warming sun, and the chirping of busy birds in the garden. Normally Oliveira would have been enjoying the early days of his favorite season, even with a heavy head. But he had just read the police report, still open in front of him.

Local Cascais fishermen found a body in their nets early that morning. It must have been in the water for a month or more. The sea worms ravaged it and the photos of the corpse were enough to churn even a veteran's stomach. Much to his disgust, he knew he would have to examine the body at the morgue before lunch.

He picked up the file and reviewed what they knew already. The deceased was fully clothed and still had his wallet and driver's license. His wallet was still full of cash, so they could rule out robbery. He was an American from New York, aged forty-four. He entered Portugal on January 8.

The US Embassy was already informed, and they replied that he was a successful fiction writer. He was a bit of a celebrity, which complicated the case for Oliveira. He really had to investigate every angle, as the embassy would require a full report from him.

His communications assistant was preparing a statement for the evening news. Fortunately for the laminated driver's license, they could use that as any current photo of the corpse's face would only horrify the viewers. The news report would end with a plea to the general public for anyone who knew the deceased to come forth with what they know.

In the meantime, he put off the visit to the city morgue to give more time for the autopsy to complete. His first stop was the Baia Hotel, an unimaginative lodging with a breathtaking view of the Cascais fishing harbor and beach immediately below it. He reviewed the hotel guest registrations and found that the deceased stayed there when he first arrived.

The older hotel manager was nervous and very reluctant to disclose anything but the obvious facts to the police. Decades under the fascist Salazar made many Portuguese very reluctant to have any interaction with the authorities.

Oliveira was getting nowhere with him. On a whim he stopped at the Concierge's desk on the way out. He found a much more cooperative young man who looked just out of college.

The concierge remembered the strange American. He sorted through one of his desk drawers and found the forwarding address he was given. Oliveira knew the place. It was the old Romanian palace. But no one had lived there for over twenty-five years. It was closed up and required serious renovation. He would go take a look after lunch.

The coroner could only confirm that the cause of death was drowning approximately four to six weeks before, with no sign of violence. The body was too far gone to know anything else. The sea worms made so many holes that it looked like Swiss cheese. The stench of sea logged putrid rot made Oliveira decide to skip lunch.

Still trying to get the stench out of his nose, Oliveira took the department's locksmith with him to the location the concierge told him. The cheerful yellow walls in the early afternoon Spring sun belied the decrepit state of the building. It was on the verge of being derelict.

The large green front gate opened with a gentle push. Halfway to the front door, Oliveira stopped and noticed signs of renovation, however slight. The garden was tidied up. Many of the windows had new boards hammered across, perhaps to keep out the elements better. But what caught his eye was the set of windows tucked in the right corner that were not bricked up. That must have been where the deceased lived.

During the ten minutes the locksmith needed to pick open the front door, Oliveira lit a cigarette. Trying to expunge the cloyingly clinging stench from the morgue, he forcibly expelled the smoke through his nose. With a loud click, the locksmith opened the door, allowing the sun light to dispel the dark gloom of the foyer.

Someone had cared for this part of the mansion. The furniture and walls of the intervening salons were clean and dusted. The lingering fragrance of the burnt wood in the enormous marble fireplace indicated it was used within the last few months.

They arrived at the apartment that corresponded with the unblocked windows that were visible from the outside. While the locksmith struggled with the apartment door, Oliveira continued farther down the dark corridor. He tried a few of the doors, but they were all locked. He went upstairs and noticed a door open at the far end.

He quietly approached, not wanting to alert who may be there. This large set of rooms was empty of anyone. Dusty white sheets covered the rich, stately furniture. The royal emblem of the defunct Romanian monarchy hung above the head of the bed. Oliveira decided that this must have been the living quarters of the king himself.

The locals claimed the king, who died in 1953, haunted the place waiting for the day he would be reinstalled on his long-abolished throne. Oliveira scoffed at the stories of banshees screaming in the night while the king walked the halls with the light of his candelabra shining intermittently through the cracked walls. Sometimes, they said, one could see him working in his garden under the full moon.

Oliveira did not believe in ghosts. He could not understand, having finally escaped this vale of woe, why anyone would want to return to the miseries of this world. The locksmith interrupted his thoughts by yelling that the door was opened.

The two-room apartment was well cared for. Clearly someone had lived there recently. Three things caught his eye. A pair of suitcases were open on the bed, packed as if the owner planned to leave at a moment's notice. A handwritten journal laid open on the desk. He put on his gloves and took it to be translated as he neither spoke nor read English. Also laying on the desk was a new barely used US passport.

Back at his office, he filed his findings and gave the journal to the department translator. He handed the passport to his assistant to glean anything useful from it. He busied himself by reviewing the report for the national news networks for later that evening. Oliveira hoped that the plea at the end with the deceased's photo would be heeded and new information revealed.

The next morning again found Oliveira leaning back in his chair, staring at the ceiling with the file opened before him. He pondered the latest pieces of the puzzle. He found the deceased's apartment. He appeared to be preparing for a trip. And then, there was his journal.

Pressure from the US embassy would suffice to put his journal at the head of the translation line, but translating handwriting is particularly time-consuming. The journal may be all that he needed to close the case, or it may only be the plot of a new novel. The deceased was supposedly a renowned author. What was truly strange was how he found that place and why did he choose to live there.

A policeman from the precinct reception knocked on his door, interrupting his thoughts. He showed in the manager of the Deck Bar. He had information that may be useful. The news report of the night before appeared to be having results. Oliveira motioned to the empty chair in front of his desk. A stenographer sat at another table to copy what was spoken.

The manager remembered the American ate dinner there often. The only notable thing he could remember was that the deceased always drank a lot at dinner and often left rather tipsy. A waiter, who spoke good English, interacted with him every time. They seemed quite friendly with each other.

Unfortunately, the waiter left for his annual vacation. He was due back three weeks ago but has disappeared after the mysterious death of his wife. Oliveira recognized the waiter's name as a person of interest in the case being handled by his colleague.

Oliveira thanked him for being a good citizen of the new Republic and told the young policeman still standing by the door to take him down the hall to Detective Sousa. The manager might shed some light on the case of the missing waiter's wife.

Ah! So, he liked to drink. We have something in common. He murmured to himself. So, something did come out of the brief interview with the manager. Perhaps the deceased drank too much, fell into the sea, and drowned? But the US Embassy would need proof of that, and the corpse was too far gone to have any traces of blood with alcohol in it. Nonetheless, it was something to consider.

The next day, the coroner called Oliveira and informed him that his report would include nothing more than what he had told him before. He asked what to do with the body. Oliveira replied that he had to think about it and would get back to him with an answer.

Oliveira asked his assistant, Jose, if there was any emergency contact information in the passport he found in the deceased's apartment. Jose answered that indeed there was a woman's name and phone number of such a contact. Oliveira told him to take the passport to the translation department and tell them to call the woman mentioned in the deceased's passport to ask what should be done with the body.

Later that day, a bartender from the Estoril Casino was ushered into his office. He had not much to add except that there was a regular patron who seemed to be friends with the deceased. The bartender remembered that they often discussed a love interest of his.

A love interest? Oliveira decided he had to meet the patron that evening. He asked the bartender if the deceased would drink too much. The bartender replied that all his patrons drank too much.

Later that night, Oliveira took one of his junior partners with him to the casino bar. The bartender motioned with his eyes toward the knowledgeable patron. Oliveira approached the urbane, well-dressed elderly man and showed him his detective badge. The patron's face lit up in fear. He tried to run for the exit, but the junior detective tackled him to the ground and put hand cuffs on him.

In front of the other lethargic patrons and casino staff, it was quite a show. They pushed him into the backseat of the police car and returned to the precinct. They searched his pockets and found his French ID card. After a quick research, they discovered he was wanted by the French and Spanish police for arms smuggling to the Corsican and Basque separatists.

Pierre Le Petit was his name. He was self-righteously outraged by his treatment, barely able to contain himself as he squirmed in the chair in front of Oliveira. Once he understood what Oliveira wanted, he stopped his French expletives and said nothing more. Thinking he was a suspect in the murder of his oft-time American drinking partner, he refused to cooperate. Oliveira told him he would sit in a jail cell until either the French or Spanish police called for his extradition. He would be extradited to whomever answered first.

Le Petit responded by placing a card on Oliveira's desk. "Call this number. Everything will be cleared up."

Oliveira answered, "I will call no one until you answer my questions regarding the deceased: what you know about him and anything that might explain his death. No one suspects you did it. Then we'll see about your extradition."

Relieved that he was not considered a suspect, Le Petit explained everything he knew concerning the strange American, which mainly centered on the even stranger 'Only After Dark', as the deluded deceased called her. He described the strange rituals of the sex cult and how completely obsessed the fool had become.

Le Petit tried to warn him to get a grip. She was clearly manipulating him, but for what aim Le Petit could not fathom. They would meet at various decrepit mansions in Estoril, which she apparently was trying to get ready for sale for her family.

He was not sure if anything she told the enthralled American was true. But there was no talking sense to him. Perhaps, he speculated, she spurned him, and he killed himself over it. The last time they met, the American was past being inebriated and was supposed to meet her later.

After nearly a half an hour of Le Petit's bizarre account with Oliveira's clarifying questions, Le Petit fell back into silence with a repeated request to call the phone number on the card. Oliveira, thinking it would be someone such as an internal security officer in a foreign embassy, picked up the card.

"Who is this?"

"Inspector, did you ever fight in any of the colonial wars?"

"Twelve years as an officer in the counter-insurgency special forces in Guinea-Bissau. Why do you ask?"

"Ah, Guinea-Bissau, the most difficult of your colonial foes. Did you ever ask yourself why the Portuguese army in Guinea was better supplied with US-made weapons and ordinance than your fellow soldiers in Angola and Mozambique?"

"I didn't question anything in those days."

"As you now know, I am a private arms supplier. After the US stopped supplying your country with military weapons and ammunition that were to be used in your colonial wars, a certain Portuguese acquaintance introduced me to an important military officer leading the counter-insurgency forces in Guinea. Do I have your attention?"

"Yes, but where do you come into the picture?"

"Well, my business requires contacts all over the world. Because of my own time as a Major General fighting a desperate counterinsurgency war for my country, France, in Vietnam, I had built up many important contacts that became especially useful when South Vietnam became flooded with every manner of US military hardware. I just connected the dots."

"OK, fine. Whose phone number is this? And why should I believe you?"

"You might have heard of him during your time there: Carlos Fabião."

"Carlos Fabião?" Oliveira sputtered. "Colonel Carlos Alberto Idães Soares Fabião?"

"Yes, the very same. You can confirm it by calling him. It's late enough. He should be home. Ask him for advice about what to do with me."

Oliveira sat back and stared at the spot on the ceiling that always holds his attention in perplexing moments like this. Colonel Fabião was the commanding officer of the Portuguese Army in Guinea during Oliveira's time there, and a member of the revolutionary junta in 1974 after the overthrow of the fascist government.

He considered what to do. It indeed was too late to be calling at home one of the most influential men of his country. Should he call anyway? Should he keep Le Petit locked up until he could call the number the next day? That would surely infuriate him. He would certainly relay his treatment to the Colonel. How would the Colonel react to that, specifically to Oliveira? What to do? What to do?

Finally, Oliveira's well-tested sense of self-preservation decided on his best course of action. He had what he needed from the wanted Frenchman. "Ok, fine. I don't need to call him now. I'll confirm this phone number tomorrow. My assistant here will drive you back to the casino or your home. If you're lying, we'll find you."

The assistant escorted Le Petit out and away. Oliveira threw Le Petit's card into the trash bin.

The next morning found Oliveira again staring at the ceiling with the transcript of his conversation with Le Petit open in front of him. There was a new person of interest, a curious Only After Dark. What kind of name was that? How could he find her? A sex cult, too?

He had two more pieces of the puzzle, but where to put them? How to place them with the others? His thoughts were interrupted by a knock on his door.

"The US Embassy is on the phone asking about the case of the deceased American. What to tell them?"

"Tell them I'm still diligently working on it and have made no conclusions."

Five minutes later, the young translator who was always flirting with him entered his office and sat down, as if she owned the chair in front of his desk. After some small talk, she got around to the point of her visit.

"I contacted the woman whose number was in the deceased's passport. It was his ex-wife. I explained what happened and asked her what to do with the body. She replied he should never have divorced her. Everyone cheats on each other these days. As for his body, throw him back into the sea. Then she hung up. Do you think she meant to give him a burial at sea?"

So, he recently divorced his cheating wife and had not changed his emergency contact yet. That seems important. Oliveira murmured. She started to share with him the details what she did over the last weekend and asked hopefully if he had no plans for the next one. She clearly did not intend to leave any time soon. He impatiently pointed to the door. She gave a hurtful pout and left.

It was probably true that having a woman in his life might pull him out of his funk. But the wrong one would only make things worse. Besides, she rubbed him the wrong way, too flighty, too chatty. The woman he preferred would be much more serious and talked little. As chance would have it, the exact same woman knocked on his door almost ten minutes later. She was the recently divorced assistant to the coroner.

"What should we do with the American's body, Senor Inspector Oliveira?"

"Tell our communications office to call the US Embassy and ask them what to do with it. Inform them his ex-wife does not want to cooperate. Why don't you have a seat and chat for a while? It's been a long time since we last had a chance to catch up."

"Senor Inspector, I know what you're thinking, but my divorce has been too recent. Perhaps I'll finally get over my bastard ex-husband running off with our babysitter, but I'm not there yet. I have to get back." She abruptly turned and left.

Ah, it's just as well. I could never get used to my woman always smelling of formaldehyde and death. He sighed and leaned back to stare at his favorite spot on the ceiling, trying to gather his thoughts.

He pieced together what he knew so far. The deceased recently divorced his cheating wife and came to Portugal to drive her from his mind. He was open to another relationship quickly to distract him from his recently failed one, as most men would do in the same situation.

He found a mysterious woman who captured his heart. He became completely infatuated with her. That she was a member, or even the leader, of a sex cult certainly helped that process. He often drank too much, probably because his deep emotional wound was not healed. But how did he become food for sea worms? There was still a wide chasm to cross to find that answer.

After a weekend of pondering, the chasm was no less wide the next Monday morning. Leaning back in his chair, somewhat hung over, Oliveira considered that maybe he was at a dead end. Clearly the strange woman, Only After Dark, was key to determining what really happened. But he had no photo of her, did not know her real name, no address. In short, he knew nothing about her. Searching for her would be completely futile.

Maybe the translation of his journal could reveal some important clues? He walked over to the translation department to see how things were progressing. It was glacial. The deceased's handwriting was terrible. The translator concentrated on the outline that filled the latter half of the notebook. It appeared to be an outline for a novel. But every other sentence was impossible to decipher. It might be weeks. It would be much faster if they hired a handwriting specialist who was a native speaker to type it into readable English.

Where could he find such a person? He told them to do their best to get it done as soon as possible. He went for lunch. When he returned to his office, a middle-aged woman was sitting patiently on the waiting bench outside with her purse on her lap staring at the wall straight ahead. She was the city librarian, who had a strange request from the deceased.

About two months earlier, he had asked her to research a topic that required her to go to the library at the University of Coimbra. She repeated every detail that he had told her. This, combined with what Le Petit described, elaborated this mysterious piece of the puzzle.

She had Oliveira's undivided attention. When she paused, he urged her to continue. "Thank you. Now please tell me what you found in your research."

The Fox Spirit is an ancient cult found in northern China and Japan. This spirit takes the form of a beautiful young woman who appears to a man sleeping in bed at night and seduces him. Once the seduction is consummated, she departs with his soul, leaving a dead husk behind. There are small shrines throughout the forests of these regions dedicated by wives to appease the Fox Spirit to not seduce and take away their husbands just because she can.

From what the deceased told her, it appeared that rather than shunning her, the statue was meant to invite the sinister spirit into their presence. Her larger-than-life likeness, as he described it, was not Asian at all. It was closer to a strange western erotic ideal often found in the Art Nouveau era.

Her conclusion of the significance of the fox was that the result definitely was not positive for the man. Perhaps the woman who invited him imagined herself to be a fox spirit or possessed by one. Perhaps she intended to possess him somehow, but to what end the librarian could not imagine. Oliveira thanked her for her great help and escorted her to the main precinct door.

Oliveira had to reread several times the notes the stenographer took of their conversation before he could try to make sense of what he had just heard. It seemed that it was no longer a simple case of a vulnerable, jilted lover committing suicide. But how to proceed? Did she poison or suffocate him with a pillow and throw the body into the sea? Did she simply push him into the ocean late at night, knowing he could not swim? The terrible state of the cadaver would reveal nothing. How could he find this woman?

He decided to have the case mentioned again on the evening news, hoping that someone else might appear with another piece of the puzzle. If nothing materialized by the following Monday, he would have to write up a report of what he knew and submit it as an unsolved death, likely a suicide. It was already Tuesday. That would give the public six days to come forth with new knowledge. His chief was becoming impatient for the case to end, no matter how frustrating the conclusion might be.

It was late Monday afternoon on the very day of the deadline when a bedraggled young man was shown into his office, poorly dressed with dark rings of insomnia under his eyes. Oliveira invited the clearly distraught man to sit down and tell him what he knew.

The young man asked him in a hoarse near whisper if he had a few hours because what he had to tell would take that long. Oliveira reassured him he had all the time in the world, if he would only speak louder.

"OK. I'll try, sir. Maybe a cup of coffee would help, a double, if that is not too much trouble. I have not been sleeping well since I met him."

Oliveira nodded to his assistant to make double espressos for everyone and motioned for the stenographer to begin.

"The night before the fishermen found that body in the nets, I had a nasty argument with my wife and her obnoxious mother. I took a walk on the Paredão to calm my seething anger. Finally, I sat down on a bench overlooking the ocean. It was about eleven at night. What happened next has robbed me of my peace of mind and any possibility of much sleep since then.

"After a while, a man sat down beside me, a foreigner who spoke English with an American accent. He was dressed in normal street clothes, but they were soaking wet. Despite the winter wind, he was barefoot. He gave out a long, hollow, eerie sigh and told me the strangest story. This is what he said:

How I love the wild winter waves crashing at my feet! My 'love' is not like others who really mean 'like', as in "I really love your hair". No, when I love, it is with such intensity and passion that it overwhelms me. I completely surrender to its power...

FINAL THOUGHTS

Inspector Oliveira thanks you very much for reading the account of his very odd case and he trusts you were intrigued by it. This is the result of a lot of hard work. He asks you, dear reader, to please leave a thoughtful and considerate review on Amazon. These are especially important to the author. If you ctrl + click on the link below or copy and paste it into your browser, you will be taken directly to the book review page.

https://www.amazon.com/review/create-review?asin=1735260673

Also, please leave a review on www.goodreads.com:

ABOUT THE AUTHOR

Born in Philadelphia, Thomas Murray is foremost a storyteller and has been writing all his life. He was a published member of the San Francisco Poet's Union and winner of Bay Area poetry and short story awards. He currently lives in Portugal.

Having lived on 5 continents for over 25 years and traveled to 89 countries, he has trained his mind to be sensitive to the wide range of nuances that make up the personalities of everyone he meets. Appreciating global cultures is fundamental to everything he writes. He includes many details about the places and characters to make the readers feel they are part of the story.

When he is not writing, he is travelling and learning foreign languages, currently Portuguese.

You can learn more about the author and his writing at https://www.thomasmurraywriter.com/

Please like his Facebook page:
https://www.facebook.com/thmurraywriter

You can contact the author at Bastet Publishing: info@bastet.ink

A recent photo of the author overlooking the ocean by Estoril
for an article about him in the Portuguese news magazine, Visão.

Also by the Same Author

The Eye of the Beholder, Bastet Publishing, 2020 (first in the Gwendolyn series)

A young art forger on the run …

Gwendolyn, a likable rogue with attitude, is secretly a successful fine-art forger rubbing shoulders with society's elite and shady art dealers. When she switches her painting with the original in a private home and escapes, she is confident with another successful heist. Until the next day when the owners are found murdered.

Framed for murder, she must travel to dangerous exotic lands to find the real murderers and clear her name. But as she delves deeper into the dangerous underworld of art forgery and betrayal, she realizes that she may be in over her head.

As the stakes get higher and her enemies close in, Gwendolyn must use all her cunning and skill to survive. Will she be able to untangle the web of lies and clear her name? Or will she become the next victim in a deadly game of cat and mouse?

https://www.amazon.es/dp/1735260606

Red Is a Color, Bastet Publishing, 2024 (second in the Gwendolyn series)

Is it a crime to be a redhead?

Gwendolyn, our favorite art forger and seductress extraordinaire, returns for another hair-raising adventure. Set in the sensuous backdrop of Portugal, Gwendolyn's latest project starts off as just another painting to forge and another wealthy eccentric to con. But as she delves deeper into the lifestyle of her unsuspecting mark, she begins to uncover more questions than answers.

How did he acquire a previously unknown Renaissance masterpiece by Botticelli? Why does he spend every evening worshipfully gazing at his personal goddess of love? Who is his tempestuous friend with an evil obsession with redheads? Who are the fanatical cultists trailing her every move?

The shadows of reality and myth blur, threatening to swallow her up in a deadly abyss... Will she survive this latest escapade with her life, much less her sanity intact?

www.amazon.com/dp/B0D64LM15C

The Adventures of Nuno and Figo: An Illustrated Journey of Two Unlikely Friends, Bastet Publishing, 2020 (first in the Gwennie series)

One clever rat, one tramp steamship, one hungry lynx …

Experience an adventure unlike any other. Follow Nuno, a clever Iberian Lynx, as he embarks on a treacherous journey to Southern California in search of a new life. Along the way, he meets Figo, a streetwise ship rat, who introduces him to the different cultures, music, and cuisines of the ports they visit.

Together, they face perils lurking around every corner as they form an unlikely friendship. Will it endure the journey, or will the dangers of California prove too difficult to survive? With beautiful illustrations by Madalena Bastos, this is a book you won't want to miss. The author will donate 10% of net proceeds to one or several organizations whose mission is to save the wonderful Iberian Lynx.

https://www.amazon.es/dp/1735260622

The Amazing Tale of Gwennie: Homeless to Palace, Bastet Publishing, 2022 (second and last in the Gwennie series)

From homeless cat to palace queen…

How did Gwennie journey from being a forlorn homeless cat in southern California to being the spoiled queen of a palace in Portugal? As the daughter of Nuno, an Iberian Lynx, and Terpsie, a Maine Coon cat, this (mostly) true story continues as the second in the series that started with The Adventures of Nuno and Figo: The Incredible Journey of Two Unlikely Friends (Illustrated).

Gwennie travels to even more exotic places than her famous father. Follow her journey as she incredibly ends up in Portugal, the same country as her father's homeland, a half a world away.

https://www.amazon.es/dp/B0BCS7NNBX

Ponce de León: A Modern Sequel, Bastet Publishing, 2022

What is the meaning of life if you can live forever?

What if 500 years ago Ponce de León did discover the Fountain of Youth? He and his crew have everything anyone could dream of: wealth, health, love of friends, and time; eternal time. But is immortality a blessing or a curse? Ponce de Léon is not so sure. He enters a personal crisis seeking this answer to the meaning of life. His search for answers leads him to a truth he never expected.

https://www.amazon.es/dp/173526069X